BLANK SLATE

SHANELL KEYS

Copyright © 2022 Shanell Keys.

All rights reserved. No part of this book may be reproduced, stored, or transmitted by any means—whether auditory, graphic, mechanical, or electronic—without written permission of both publisher and author, except in the case of brief excerpts used in critical articles and reviews. Unauthorized reproduction of any part of this work is illegal and is punishable by law.

ISBN: 979-8-88640-568-2 (sc)
ISBN: 979-8-88640-569-9 (hc)
ISBN: 979-8-88640-570-5 (e)

Because of the dynamic nature of the Internet, any web addresses or links contained in this book may have changed since publication and may no longer be valid. The views expressed in this work are solely those of the author and do not necessarily reflect the views of the publisher, and the publisher hereby disclaims any responsibility for them.

One Galleria Blvd., Suite 1900, Metairie, LA 70001
1-888-421-2397

CHAPTER 1

It was a day like any other, or at least I thought it was, but it was the day that would change my life forever. I can still remember it so vividly it seems like yesterday. It was a warm spring day, almost too warm. I knew if it was that warm already, we were in for a hot summer. I was already sweating terribly when I arrived at Sacramento Grace Hospital, where I worked as a nurse. I took my cell phone out of my pocket to check the time. Eight fifteen. I could still stop by the cafeteria for some coffee. Even though they had coffee at the nurse's station, it wasn't nearly as good as the coffee in the cafeteria. I took the elevator to the second floor and went down the long hallway to the cafeteria. As soon as I entered, Mac looked up and smiled. He had worked in the cafeteria for years, and he had become a good friend of mine. He knew what I wanted even before I told him my order.

"Hi, Jen. Iced white mocha, right?"

I nodded. "You know me too well."

Mac started working on my drink while I got the money from my purse. I knew it would be a dollar fifty with tax. I looked around the cafeteria, which was already buzzing with activity. There were people of all ages scattered around the tables and booths. One little girl, who couldn't have been more than two, was smearing syrup all over a table, much to the disapproval of the woman she was with, her mother, probably. The woman quickly snatched her up and carried her to the ladies' room, scolding her the whole way. It reminded me of when my own son was that age. In some ways it seemed so long ago; in other ways it felt like only yesterday.

"Here's your drink." Mac handed it to me over the counter. "That will be a dollar fifty."

I handed him the money and took a sip of my drink. "Have a good day, Mac."

"You, too." He started humming a song I couldn't recognize as he turned to help the next customer.

* * * *

"Hey, Jen!" Lisa called as I arrived at my station a short while later. Lisa was one of those overly perky people. Although she could be annoying at times, she was a nice person and an even better nurse. She really cared about her patients, and it showed. She always went the extra mile to let them know they were more than just a patient. I had learned a lot from working with her the past few years.

"So, who do we have today?" I asked, browsing through the patients' files.

"Well, only one new patient since yesterday. But this one is really interesting. Some guy was in a car accident, and the car was totaled. Besides a little bump on the head, he's fine, physically. But he can't remember anything."

"He can't remember anything?" I repeated.

She nodded. "He came in around midnight. So far, no one's claiming him. And he didn't have any type of identification on him. News cameras have already been here to cover the story. It was quite a zoo all morning. They are calling him 'the mystery man.' He's cute, too." She grinned, and I had to laugh. Lisa loved men, especially ones that she considered hot. I always tried to see beyond just outward appearance. I felt that it was much more important to have a kind heart than a six pack. "Oh, and Mrs. Furguson is here again," Lisa continued. "She's complaining of leg pain. You can take care of her, and then our mystery man." She winked and handed me both patients' files.

Mrs. Furguson was one of our regular patients, a sweet old lady in her late eighties. She was always coming in with some kind of ailment, but everyone knew she needed company more than she needed medical care. Her husband had passed away a few years back, and her children didn't visit much. She was healthy as an ox, but we would always check her vitals just to humor her. We weren't really supposed to treat patients that weren't admitted to the hospital, but there was an unspoken understanding when it came to Mrs. Furguson. I took one last sip of my coffee before I headed for the exam room.

"Hi, Mrs. Furguson, what seems to be the problem today?" I sat down in the chair across from her, and she looked at me with a sweet smile. Her silver hair fell into wispy curls around her face, and I could tell that she had been really pretty in her younger years.

"Well, my leg has been hurting a little bit." She held it up for me to see, and I reached out to touch it, pretending to examine it, even though I knew it didn't need examining.

"And when did it start hurting?"

"Just yesterday."

"Can you stretch it out like this?" I stretched my leg straight out to show her.

"I think so." She did the same with her own leg, and she seemed to have more flexibility than I did. That reminded me how badly I needed to work out! "So, how is that handsome little boy of yours?" she asked.

I smiled a proud smile, as I did when anyone asked about my child. "Danny's doing really well, but he's not so little anymore. He's nine now." I took the blood pressure cuff from its hook on the wall and slipped it over her arm before pressing the button to start it.

She looked surprised. "Nine, already? Time really flies when you're my age." Then she looked at me with a curious expression. "And what about you? Have you had any hot dates recently?"

I smiled. "I don't really have time. I'm always at work or spending time with Danny."

"Well, you should. A pretty young lady like yourself shouldn't be sitting around the house on a Saturday night."

I smiled. "I will try my best to take your advice, okay?" The blood pressure monitor beeped to let me know it was done, and I glanced at the numbers. "One twenty over seventy two. Perfect." I slipped it off her arm and placed it back on the hook. "Now, I want you to take one of these every day, and your leg should be feeling better in a jiffy." I reached into the drawer, and pulled out a small pill bottle. It was actually vitamins, but she didn't know that. It made her feel as if we were doing something to help her, so we always kept them stocked in the exam room.

"Thank you," she said. "You really are the sweetest nurse I've ever had."

"You're very welcome," I told her. I helped Mrs. Furguson walk out the door and looked at the file of my next patient. The mystery man. On his file they called him John Doe. He had been picked up by the ambulance after some kindhearted person had called and reported seeing him in a ditch. He had a mild concussion, but other than that he was in good shape. I thought to myself how confusing it would be to not know who you were. I walked to room 220 and slowly opened the door, knocking softly as I did so.

"Hello?" I saw him sitting in the hospital bed. His TV was on, tuned to Jeopardy! but instead of watching it he was staring blankly into space. I thought that it felt strange not to know his real name. I didn't know what to call him. "Hi, sir. I'm Nurse Jennifer. I'll be taking care of you today."

He looked up at me, and I saw then how truly lost he looked. He was handsome, just as Lisa had said. He had wavy, dark hair and big green eyes. He was tall, and I noticed that his feet almost hung off the end of the hospital bed. But there was something about his eyes—they looked so sad, and I felt bad for him. He had a bandage on his forehead, and I could see that it needed changing. "Hi," he replied. "You can call me John; that's what everyone else is calling me."

"Okay, John, nice to meet you." I was trying to sound as cheerful as possible, hoping it might help to boost his mood. "Let's get you a clean bandage." I went to the supply cabinet at the far end of the room, and pulled out a large cloth bandage and some tape. "Are you ready? This might sting a little." He nodded and leaned toward me, and I quickly pulled off the old bandage and applied some ointment. Then I covered it with a new one and taped it up. His cut wasn't as bad as I thought it would be, but I knew that head injuries always bled a lot.

"You're really good; I didn't even feel that."

"Thanks, I've been doing this a really long time." I smiled at the compliment. "So, tell me how your pain is, on a scale from one to ten."

He shrugged. "My head still hurts, but I'm kind of used to it now. I guess about a four or five." I nodded and jotted it down on his chart.

"So tell me something," he said, looking serious. I looked up from his chart. "Sure."

"Have you ever treated someone like me? A freak who can't even remember his own name?"

"No. But there's a first time for everything. And don't call yourself a freak."

He was silent for a moment before he continued. "Does it say in my chart that my car crashed into a ditch?" I nodded and then sat down in the chair beside him. I could tell he had more to say. "I just wonder what I was doing.

I mean, it's like I just lost control and skidded off the road. And I can't remember anything before the accident. Nothing. I have been lying here in this bed trying so hard to remember something, but there's nothing. Do you know how frustrating that is?"

I was at a loss for words. Of course I had no idea what it would be like to forget everyone, everything, in my life.

"You don't have to answer that. Nobody could understand what I'm going through." He looked down, shaking his head sadly.

I patted him on the shoulder sympathetically. "Just relax. Hopefully, as soon as the swelling goes down, you will start to regain your memory."

"What if I don't? What if I never remember?"

"Try not to worry about that right now. Just concentrate on getting better, okay? I know it's easier said than done. I've done a lot of research on amnesia, and at some point, most patients do regain their memory."

He nodded, quietly taking that in. "Most, but not all, right?"

"Yes. But like I said, you should just rest, and take care of yourself." There was some awkward silence after that, but it was interrupted when Doctor Martin entered the room. I stood up, trying not to look too comfortable. He was the lead doctor in our department, and I had never really liked him much. He had the bedside manor of an ogre. He cared more about billing insurance agencies for unnecessary tests than he did about the patients.

"Hello, sir. I'm Doctor Martin. It's time to take you in for more tests." John just sighed, and I slowly made my way to the door.

"Okay, I have to get going. It was nice meeting you, John." I said with a smile.

He looked up, and for the first time, he smiled. "Nice to meet you, too, Jennifer."

CHAPTER 2

By the time I arrived to pick up Danny from his after-school program, I was tired and weary from a long day on my feet. I couldn't wait to get home and relax a little. There were children everywhere, loading into cars and minivans. Most of them seemed happy, with big smiles on their faces. But not Danny. He walked to the car with his head hanging down, looking depressed. Although he was nine, he was small for his age, and he looked much younger. He was often made fun of at school, and I worried about him all the time. He didn't have many friends, and while most of the boys his age were into sports, he was more of a bookworm. He would spend hours in his room, reading. I never complained, because he was truly the most easygoing kid I could hope for. He was just misunderstood, and I wished other people could see him the way I did.

"Hi, Danny, how was your day?" I asked cheerfully.

He shrugged. "Okay, I guess."

"Why the long face?" I felt silly as soon as the words slipped out of my mouth. I knew perfectly well what was wrong with Danny. It was his weekend to go to his father's house, and he hated going there. My ex-husband wasn't the most devoted father. He had him every other weekend but not because he wanted to. He had walked out on us when

Danny was just a baby. Only six months later, he had remarried, to the woman he'd had an affair with. Since then, they'd had two children together, a boy and a girl. When Danny was with his father, he was treated like an outcast. If anything bad ever happened, it was always Danny's fault. And his father was always trying to get him to be more like his other son, who was a little-league champion. Danny had never been into sports, and I doubted he ever would be. I wished his father could just accept him for who he was.

"How about we stop for some ice cream today? It sure is hot." I looked at Danny for a response, but he just shrugged.

"Sure."

"Listen, Danny, I know you don't like going to your dad's, but it could be worse. At least you only have to go every other weekend."

"I don't see why I have to go there at all. He never does anything with me anyway. All he cares about is Max's games or Megan's dance recitals." He looked sadly down at his feet.

"I know, pal. How about we do something special next weekend? There's a new wild animal park we could go to."

He cracked a faint little smile. I've always loved how his eyes light up when he smiles. He loves animals, and I knew that would do the trick—for now, anyway.

Later, at home, I made sure Danny had all of his things together for the weekend. He just sat there, staring out the window, waiting for his dad to arrive. He looked like he was in mourning, and I thought it was sad that a weekend with his father could have such a negative impact on him. He sighed as he watched his dad pull up in the driveway. His wife, Carolyn, and their two children were in the car. Danny didn't like any of them, and from what I had heard, I couldn't blame him. Max was always picking on Danny, and Megan was always trying to get him in trouble. Of course, his father just defended them. In his eyes, Danny was just a mistake, even though he would never admit it.

"I'll get it," Danny said when the doorbell rang, and he slowly walked to the door and opened it. His father, David, stood there with a fake smile on his face.

"Hey, pal, you ready to go? We have to hurry; your brother has a game tonight. We don't want to be late." Danny nodded and went upstairs to get his things. David looked at me; his fake smile was fading. "So how have you been, Jen?"

"Fine," I answered. "But Danny isn't fine, and I want to talk to you about that."

"About what? Don't tell me you're feeding his drama again. You know, you really need to stop babying him. For Christ's sake, Jen, he'll be ten soon."

"I'm not, but he really doesn't want to go with you. I think you should try doing some things that he enjoys."

David rolled his eyes. "I'm not going to spend the weekend at the bookstore. I think Danny is the one with the problem, and you don't help him by giving in to him all the time. He should try acting like a boy instead of a sissy."

"I'm ready to go, Dad." Danny came downstairs with his bag flung over his shoulder. I could tell by the look on his face that he had heard what his father had said, even though he didn't say anything.

"Okay, let's go," David said, motioning toward the door. "Bye, Mom." Danny came and gave me a hug. "I love you."

"I love you, too." I squeezed him tight and kissed him on the cheek. "See you Sunday." I hated letting him go like this, but I didn't want to fight with David in front of Danny. David was good at turning anything into an argument. So I watched them get into the car and drive away, feeling like the most horrible mother in the world.

CHAPTER

3

I never knew what to do with myself on the weekends Danny was at his dad's house. It always seemed so quiet. One weekend out of the month, I had to work. I always liked those weekends in a way, because it made the time go by faster. This happened to be one of those weekends. Saturday morning, I turned on the news while I was getting ready. The top story seemed to be John Doe, the mystery man without a memory at Sacramento Grace Hospital. They showed his picture over and over, asking if anyone knew who he was. I thought it was sad that nobody had claimed him, and I was anxious to get to work and check on him.

When I arrived at work a little while later, I was shocked to see news reporters scattered all around the hospital. As soon as I walked through the doors, about ten microphones were shoved in my face, and ten different reporters shouted at me.

"Are you the nurse treating John Doe at this time?"

"Does he remember where he came from?"

"What is his long-term prognosis?"

"Can you tell us more about him?"

"No comment!" I said firmly, and I slipped through the double doors, where only hospital personnel were allowed. I was going to have to take the back way to work. I thought about how John must feel being harassed by the media. He had enough of his own emotions to deal with right now. But then it occurred to me that it was really the only way he would ever be reunited with his family. If it weren't for TV, they might never know where he was. I practically ran up the stairs to the nurses' station, where Lisa sat sipping her coffee.

"What's with all of the news reporters?" I was panting, out of breath from running up the stairs.

Lisa laughed. "We have the top story right now. Tomorrow, they will probably move on to someone else. Hey, I never had the chance to ask you what you thought of him. He's pretty cute, right?"

I shrugged. "I guess so. But he's also our patient. Our job is to treat him, not rate his cuteness. How's he doing, anyway?"

"Fine, for someone who can't remember who he is."

I grabbed his file and headed for his room. He was sitting in the chair beside his bed, watching some comedy show I didn't recognize. "Good morning, John. How are you?"

He looked up at me and smiled. "I'm okay. A little annoyed with all of the reporters."

"Sorry about that. I guess you're going to be famous for a while."

He sighed. "I would give up being famous if I could just remember something."

"Don't worry; it will all come to you," I said as I grabbed the blood pressure cuff and slipped it over his arm.

"I hope so. I'm supposed to be released in a couple of days, and I have no idea what I'm going to do."

The blood pressure monitor beeped, and I removed it from his arm. "You're all normal."

He laughed. "Am I really? I don't feel normal right now."

"Is anyone really normal?" I asked. "I think everyone has their own problems."

He considered that for a moment before he spoke again. "So what kind of problems do you have, if you don't mind me asking? Maybe someone else's problems will make mine not seem so big."

I felt strange talking to him about my personal life, but I sat in the chair across from him, and I sighed before I continued. "Well, my ex-husband, for one thing. He treats my son horribly, and he isn't very nice to me, either. But I have to deal with him because we have a child together."

"You have a son?" He looked surprised.

"Yes."

"How old?"

"Nine. He'll be ten in September." He sat there for a moment, looking shocked. "Why does that surprise you so much?" I asked.

"Because you don't look old enough to be someone's mother. Especially a nine-year-old."

I laughed. "You know, you aren't going to get any special treatment for trying to flatter me like that. I have to treat all of my patients equally. And speaking of my other patients, I'd better go check on them."

"Okay." He sounded a little disappointed.

"Don't worry; I will be here if you need me," I said playfully. "Just press the little button, okay?" He nodded, and I headed down the hall to check on my next patient.

Melissa was a cancer patient who had been with us off and on for a little over a year. She had been married just a few months when she'd been diagnosed. She had been through a lot of treatments, with horrible side effects, but through it all she'd kept such a positive attitude. I'd always admired her. It was patients like Melissa that made me love my job.

"Hi, Melissa," I said as I entered her room. Her husband, Jack, sat beside her bed, holding her hand. And, as always, she had a big smile on her face. They were a cute couple, and it was clear how much they loved each other.

"Hi, Jen." Although she was always happy, she seemed especially giddy today.

"You're in a good mood today," I said as I slipped the blood pressure cuff over her arm.

"I am." She looked at Jack, beaming. "Should we tell her the good news, sweetie?"

He smiled. "Sure."

I laughed. "I can't stand the suspense."

"We're pregnant!" she squealed. "We just found out. We weren't exactly trying, with all the treatments I'm doing right now, but we're pleasantly surprised. The oncologist is supposed to come in later to discuss my treatment options, but I am optimistic."

"Well, that is good news!" I said. "And it's a good thing you told me, too. I was going to give you your medication, but you might want to discuss it with your doctor. Some aren't safe during pregnancy. Now, let's get your temperature, and I will leave the two of you alone."

She nodded, and I jotted her blood pressure reading and temperature on her chart. As I took care of the rest of my patients that afternoon, I thought about the day I had found out I was pregnant with Danny. I had been at work when I realized I was a little late, so I went down to the pharmacy during my break and picked up a pregnancy test. Things weren't exactly great between David and me, and I worried about how he might react if I was pregnant. We had decided to wait another year before we started a family. As I stood in the ladies' room with the positive pregnancy test in my hand, I was more scared than I'd ever been in my life. And later that evening, when I told David he was going to be a father, he'd yelled and lectured me for what seemed like hours. "I thought we had decided to wait!" he'd screamed. "How could you do this to me?" As if getting pregnant was something I had done to him.

The day I gave birth to Danny, David was out of town on what I thought was a business meeting. But I found out later he was shacked up with Carolyn in a hotel somewhere. The first time I looked at my son, I fell in love with him. I knew he was special. His father didn't even meet him until he was a week old. We started fighting more and more, until we both accepted that it was over. I suspected deep down that he was spending more and more time with Carolyn. And I was right, because not long after our divorce was finalized, he married her. And soon after that, she was pregnant. Only this time he stuck around. When his other son was born he was at the hospital, snapping pictures and posting them on Facebook.

I got used to being a single mom pretty quickly. In some ways, I even liked it. There was more time for me to focus on Danny, without anyone else to worry about. I loved every minute I spent with him, and I tried to be the best mother I possibly could. But still, sometimes I wished he had a father figure in his life. Someone who loved him as much as I did. Someone who loved me just as much.

CHAPTER 4

Sunday evening, I waited for Danny to come home. I was busy making the fixings for his favorite meal, tacos. I always felt the need to do something nice for him after he had spent the weekend at his dad's. I grabbed a beer from the fridge and sipped on it as I grated the cheese. I always loved the way a nice cold beer tasted with tacos. I stirred the taco meat again impatiently and tasted it to make sure it was just right. Finally, I saw the car pull into the driveway. Danny jumped out, his bag flung over his shoulder. He ran toward the house. David pulled out of the driveway and sped away, as if he couldn't wait to be free of Danny, to get back to his real family.

"Hi, Mom!" Danny called as he came through the door.

"Hi, son. How was your weekend?"

He shrugged. "All right, I guess. Max's team won, so Dad was in a good mood all weekend. What's for dinner?"

"Tacos. The crunchy ones—your favorite."

He grinned from ear to ear. "Yum! I'm starved."

That evening we talked and laughed as we ate. Danny told me about his weekend, and I was glad to know he hadn't had such a horrible time. It made me feel a little better about making him go to his father's house. After dinner we did the dishes together, just as we always did. Then

Danny went to his room to read his new book he'd been excited about. He loved to read, but he never read when he was at his dad's house. He was afraid David would think he was a sissy, which was probably true. I flipped on the news while I finished cleaning up a bit around the house. The news reporter was standing in front of the hospital. She was a cute, perky blonde, and I just knew the station had hired her to boost their ratings.

"Mystery man John Doe has a clean bill of health, and he will be released soon," the reporter announced. "But where will he go? With no family, no job, and no memory, it seems he has nowhere to turn. A fund has been started in his name to help him start a new life. If you would like to donate to the John Doe fund, you can make donations to the address you see here."

An address popped up on the screen, along with a picture of John, and they went on to the next story. A gang had robbed a convenience store and shot the manager, but I wasn't really listening after that. I just kept thinking about John. I remembered how lost and confused he seemed when I'd met him. I felt sorry for him, and I wished there was something I could do to help. After paying all of my own bills, I didn't really have anything left to donate. I wanted to do something, I just didn't know what. Then, as I looked out the back window, I thought of something. We had a small guest house out back. It was one of the reasons David and I had bought this house when we were first married. We figured my parents would have a place to stay when they got older. But, since then, they had moved to Florida. Now the little guest house was mostly used to store a lot of old junk, but it could easily be cleaned out. It wasn't very big, just one bedroom and one bathroom, and a small living room and kitchen. But it would still be a place for him to stay while he got his life together. It even had some old furniture in it, all in pretty decent shape. Then I thought to myself that I was being crazy. I knew nothing about this guy, so why would I even consider letting him stay in the guest house? Maybe I was just too nice for my own good. I shook those thoughts out of my head. Then I finished cleaning up around the house before I took a nice, hot bath and went to bed.

CHAPTER 5

The next day, when I arrived at work, the hospital seemed eerily quiet— no camera crews and no reporters. I had tuned in to the news while I was getting ready for work, and it seemed the new top story was the family of the convenience store worker who'd been shot and the bail hearing for the gang members who'd shot him. It was amazing how quickly things changed in the media word. But I wasn't going to complain; it was much better than being chased down with cameras and microphones. I stopped by the cafeteria to pick up a coffee before I started my rounds, checking on all of my patients.

My first stop was Melissa's room. I was always happy to check on her; she was one of my favorite patients. She had been in and out of the hospital, trying out different treatments and medications. Sometimes she was so sick she couldn't even keep down any food. But I don't think I ever saw her without a smile on her face. That positive attitude had kept me going through some of the rough times I'd had; it was contagious. After a visit with Melissa, I always left smiling too. But today she didn't seem like her old perky self. As a matter of fact, she looked depressed.

"Good morning, Melissa," I said. "How are you today?" She shrugged. "All right, I guess."

"Just all right?"

She nodded. "We talked to the doctor yesterday, and he doesn't think my body is strong enough to handle a pregnancy. He recommended that I have an abortion." She looked down sadly, and I could tell she was starting to cry.

I grabbed a box of tissues and handed her a couple. "I'm sorry, Melissa. I know you were really excited about the baby."

"I really was." The tears started streaming down her face now, and I felt as if I would cry any minute myself. "It's just not fair!" she cried, slamming her fist against the bedside table. "I've always been a good person. I didn't do anything to deserve this!" I had never seen her so angry before. I didn't know what else to do, so I sat beside her in the bed, and I put my arms around her. I hugged her for a while before she wiped her eyes and continued. "What would you do?"

"Excuse me?"

"If you were in the same situation, what would you do? The doctor says if I proceed with the pregnancy, there's only a 25 percent chance I will live. If I decide to end the pregnancy, I have a good chance. But with all of the treatments, I probably won't be able to get pregnant again."

I thought about this for a moment. I thought about Danny and how I couldn't imagine my life without him. Not long after he was born, I had been diagnosed with premature ovarian failure. It was a heartbreaking diagnosis for me, because it meant that I would probably never have another child. I'd always pictured my family with more kids, so I could relate to how Melissa was feeling. As a nurse, I really wasn't supposed to recommend anything to any patient, and I knew I could get in trouble for saying what I was about to say. But I didn't care. "I would do whatever it takes to save you, and the baby."

She nodded; a smile began to spread across her face. "And that's exactly what I'm going to do."

After I left Melissa's room, I went to check on John, but he wasn't in his room. I looked down the long hallway, thinking maybe he had gone for a walk, but he was nowhere to be found. I walked up to Lisa, who was looking over patients' files. "Have you seen John?"

"I think he's up in pediatrics," she said. "They are having a play day with the kids, and he wanted to help out."

I nodded and went toward the elevator. I got on and pushed the button to the third floor. When I arrived at my destination, the whole third floor was a buzz of activity. Children were everywhere. A clown was making balloons into animal shapes and passing them out to children. Someone else was painting faces. And sitting in a rocking chair in the corner, reading a story to a group of children, was John. He looked relaxed and happier than I had previously seen him. When he saw me, he looked up with a smile and waved. After he finished reading the story, he stood up and came over to me.

"Hi, how's my favorite nurse?"

I smiled. "I told you, you aren't going to get any special treatment from me by giving me compliments all the time."

"Well, I was only telling the truth. You are my favorite nurse. So, what brings you to the kid zone?"

"I came to check on you, but you weren't in your room, so I had to come track you down," I said playfully. "You look like you're enjoying yourself."

He nodded. "I needed a change of scenery. I figured these kids could help me forget that I can't remember, if that makes any sense."

"That makes perfect sense," I said. "I come up here sometimes when I just need a little pick-me-up. Kids are amazing, they're so resilient."

"Yes, they are." He motioned toward a little girl getting her face painted. "Jessica has spent most of her life in the hospital, but when she saw the bandage on my head, she was so concerned about my boo-boo. She sprinkled me with some magic fairy dust, so I will get better soon."

"That's really sweet." I smiled, looking around at the children, feeling grateful that Danny was so healthy. "Well, why don't we get you back up to your room? I'm supposed to take your vitals and change your bandage."

"Okay, sounds good."

We went back to John's room, where I took his vitals, changed his bandage, and wrote the necessary information on his chart. Just as I was leaving, someone from patient services entered the room. I saw on his name tag that his name was Greg. I knew that he was probably there with the discharge information. John was scheduled to be discharged tomorrow. But discharged to where? I couldn't help but listen in as Greg questioned him.

"Do you feel that you're able to live on your own?"

"Well, I will be," John answered. "All of the media has actually been very helpful. I have a bank account with money in it, and I was offered a job at a grocery store. I can start just as soon as I'm ready. But I might need a little more time—"

Greg cut him off. "We really don't have much more time. You see, the hospital needs the room. And Doctor Martin says that you are recovered enough to be discharged."

"Recovered enough?" John sounded shocked. "This is about insurance, isn't it? Since I don't have any medical insurance for the hospital to bill, I'm not worth keeping—is that right?"

"Now, calm down," said Greg. "It isn't about that."

"The hell it isn't." John got out of bed and stomped out of the room with a sigh. Greg just sat there for a minute, looking puzzled. And that's when I did the craziest thing I had ever done in my life. I followed John down the hall.

"John, wait up!" I called, but he continued storming down the hall. I ran faster to catch up to him, and he finally slowed down a little. "I heard you talking in there, and I might be able to solve your problem."

"What could you possibly do to solve my problem?" he asked with disbelief in his voice.

"Well, I know they want to discharge you tomorrow, but you don't really have a place to stay, right?"

He nodded. "That's right, but they're going to kick me out, anyway. I can't believe those jerks."

"Well, I have a little guest house you can stay in, if you want. It's small, and it could use some work. But it's all yours. At least until you get back on your feet."

He was silent for a moment, clearly in shock. "Why would you do something like that? You don't even know me."

I shrugged. "I just like to help people. I've always been that way. Call me weird."

"I don't think you're weird. That's the nicest thing anyone has done for me—I think." We both laughed. "Listen," he continued, "I want you to know I don't expect a free ride. As soon as I start working, I can pay rent."

"Well, I wasn't really worried about that," I said.

"I won't take no for an answer," he pressed. "So I can move in tomorrow?"

"Yes, you can move in tomorrow."

CHAPTER

6

When I went to pick Danny up from school that afternoon, he bounced to the car with a big grin on his face.

"Hi, Mom!" He sat beside me and flung his backpack into the back seat. "Hi, Danny! You're in a good mood today."

"I am. Our teacher handed out rewards to the kids with good grades today. I got a special certificate, a gift card to Burger Palace, and I even get to have lunch with the principal. Isn't that great, Mom? Mom?"

I found myself thinking about other things as he was talking to me, something I tried really hard not to do. I felt it was important to give Danny my full attention. "Yes, that's great, son. Listen, we need to talk about something, okay?"

"Yeah, what?"

"Well, one of my patients had a head injury, and he has amnesia."

"Am-na—what?" Danny asked with a confused expression on his face. "Amnesia. That means he can't remember anything from before. And even though his story has been all over the news, none of his family has come to claim him. Now he's going to be released tomorrow, and he needs a place to stay. So I was thinking he could stay in the guest house, just until he has some time to figure things out."

"You're bringing a patient home?"

I laughed. "Just this once. And he's a really nice guy; you'll like him. Now, we're going to have to work hard tonight to clean out the guest house and get it ready for him. Do you think you can help me with that?"

He nodded. "Sure, Mom. I can help."

For most of that evening, Danny and I cleaned and organized the guest house. We filled a huge box with items we would take to goodwill. I'd always thought it was important for Danny to know that there were people out there who were much less fortunate than we were. Every Christmas we would volunteer at a local church to serve a meal to homeless people. Danny always loved it, and he said it made him appreciate everything he had even more. When he was going through the closet, he found an old photo album and started flipping through it. I looked over his shoulder to see that the pictures were of David and me, in happier times. We were sitting on a beach somewhere, sipping margaritas, with big smiles on our faces.

"You and Dad look happy in this picture," he said.

"We were," I answered.

"What happened? I mean, how do you go from being so happy to hating each other?"

"Your father and I don't hate each other," I lied. "We just don't see eye to eye on a lot of things. And we decided that it was better for everyone if we went our separate ways instead of fighting all the time and making everyone miserable. But we both agree on one thing—we both love you." I playfully messed up his hair, and he smiled.

"This place is looking pretty good," he said proudly. He leaned back in the chair and looked around. "You know, I've always wanted to live here someday."

"Oh, really?"

"Yeah, I could have my own space, but I would still be close to you."

"That's really nice, but I bet you will feel differently in a few years." He shook his head. "No, I don't think so."

I looked at the clock, amazed at how fast time had flown. "Well, I think it's time to go fix some dinner. How about pork chops tonight?"

He smiled. "Sounds good!"

CHAPTER 7

When I arrived at my station at work the next morning, Lisa didn't seem like her usual jovial self. She stood there, looking over her patients' files. When she saw me, she looked up.

"Hi, Jen."

"You seem excited to be alive today." I said sarcastically.

"Well, Doctor Martin came by this morning, and he wants to talk to you," she said. "And he didn't look very happy. He wants you to go by his office before you start your rounds today."

I nodded. "Okay." We both knew that Doctor Martin was a jerk; he was always trying to start trouble. I headed for his office around the corner and knocked before I entered.

"Come in," he said. I peeked inside the door to see him sitting at his desk, writing something. "Hello, Jennifer, I've been waiting for you." He motioned for me to sit in the chair across from him, so I did.

"Lisa told me you wanted to see me?"

"Yes. We need to talk. You are the nurse in charge of Melissa Edwards, right?"

I nodded. "That's right, sir."

"And did you talk to her yesterday?"

I took a deep breath. "Yes, I did."

"And did you tell her to go against doctor's orders, and continue with her pregnancy?"

I squirmed in my seat, nervously tapping my fingers on the arm rest. "I didn't say that, exactly."

"Then what exactly did you say to her?" He was raising his voice now, and it made me feel like a schoolgirl in the principal's office.

"I told her that if I were in her position, I would do anything to save myself and my baby." My voice was quiet, almost a whisper.

He nodded. "Well, as you know, that is for her doctor to decide." He reached into his drawer and pulled out some x-rays, spreading them out on his desk. "These are Melissa's," he said. "Do you see this big mass here?" I nodded.

"That is a pituitary tumor on her brain. There are medications that can shrink it, but chances are they would kill the baby. If she doesn't take the medications, the tumor will continue to grow. Pregnancy hormones will only make them grow faster. At the rate they are growing, she can't afford to wait until after the duration of the pregnancy to get treatment. And that's not her only tumor; there are more. Along her spine and in her brain. Her body is in no shape to proceed with a pregnancy. So that's why her doctor recommended that she not continue with the pregnancy. Our first priority is always to the patient."

I was silent for a minute, thinking this over. "Don't you think the baby is also a patient?"

"Excuse me?"

"Now that she's pregnant, don't you think the baby also deserves to be considered?"

He shook his head. "She's only six weeks along. It's hardly a baby yet."

"But it will be," I said. "And it's Melissa's baby. With all due respect, sir, I think it's up to her to decide."

He nodded. "Exactly. But it's not up to you to influence her with your opinions. Just treat the patients, okay?"

I nodded. "Yes, sir."

"And one more thing, Jennifer. I hear you are taking John Doe home with you when he's released today."

"Yes, he's going to stay in my guest house. He doesn't have anywhere else to go, and the hospital doesn't want to keep him here any longer."

He put his head in his hands and sighed. "You know, you can't save everyone, Jen. I have learned that the hard way during my years in the medical field. If you get too emotionally involved, you are just opening yourself up to a whole lot of heartache. That's all I have to say about that. Now, get to work. Your patients are waiting."

I nodded and headed out the door, ready to take on the day.

Mrs. Furguson was my first patient, and I smiled as I greeted her. "Hello, Mrs. Furguson. How are you today?"

"Okay, I guess. But I keep forgetting things. This morning, I forgot where I left my keys. And yesterday, I was supposed to be somewhere, but I can't remember where."

"That's okay. You know, just between you and me, I forget things all the time."

She looked surprised. "Really?"

I nodded. "I think I would forget my head if it wasn't screwed on." She laughed, and then I heard her stomach growl.

"Do you remember the last time you ate?" I asked with concern.

"Yes, of course, it was just this morning, I think." She looked down at her feet, with a confused expression on her face.

I smiled. "Why don't you come with me while I check on my other patients?"

"Okay, but I don't want to be any trouble."

"You're not any trouble at all, Mrs. Furguson."

She followed me to John's room. On the way, I picked up the sack lunch I had brought that day. I figured I could get something in the cafeteria later.

She needed it more than I did.

"Hi, John, how are you today?" I asked as we entered the room. He was sitting up in bed, watching something on the food network.

"I'll be better when I'm out of here. So, are you sure it's okay if I stay in your guest house?"

I nodded. "It's fine, really. That place has been sitting empty for years. Well, I shouldn't say empty; it was filled with all of our old junk. But don't worry; we cleaned it out for you."

"Well, I can't thank you enough," he said, meaning it.

"Oh, I almost forgot. John, this is Mrs. Furguson. Mrs. Furguson, this is John."

He smiled. "Nice to meet you."

"Nice to meet you, too." She looked around with the same bewildered expression on her face.

"Mrs. Furguson, I wanted you to meet John, because he can't remember anything before his accident less than a week ago."

"Really?" she laughed. "And I thought I was bad!" We all laughed, and I motioned for her to sit in the chair at the far end of the room.

"Why don't you sit over here and eat this while I take care of John." I handed her the sack lunch; she examined the contents and smiled.

"Thank you."

CHAPTER 8

The day flew by, and before I knew it, it was almost time for my shift to end. I nervously paced the hallways and started biting my nails. I had picked up that bad habit in childhood, but now I only did it when I was really nervous. I kept thinking that I must be crazy. I knew nothing about this guy, and I was bringing him home with me. Well, not exactly home; he would have his own space in the guest house. But still, what was I thinking? Dr. Martin was right; it was stupid of me to think that I could save everybody. But something in my gut just told me I was supposed to help John.

"Well, are you ready for this?" Lisa asked as I collected my things from my locker in the staff room.

"As ready as I'll ever be." I flung my purse over my shoulder, and we both headed for John's room.

"You've got to be kidding me," were the first words out of his mouth when he saw Lisa pushing the wheelchair. "I can walk just fine."

"It's hospital procedure, Mr. Doe," Lisa said seriously. "If you want to get out of this place, you need to ride in this. Think of it as your vehicle to freedom."

He rolled his eyes. "Well, okay, since you put it that way." He climbed out of his bed and into the wheelchair. "Let's go."

Downstairs, about a hundred news reporters and cameras were waiting for us. We did our best to ignore them as they questioned us.

"Well, looks like they haven't forgotten about you, after all," I said to John. I looked over at Lisa, who was pushing his wheelchair. "I'll go pull the car up front, okay?" She nodded, and I ran past the reporters to the parking lot.

When I had pulled the car around, Lisa was waiting with John by the curb, a crowd of reporters gathered around them, trying to ask questions. John looked as if he couldn't wait to get away from them. Lisa quickly opened the door, and he jumped into the passenger seat. My heart was racing, because I had never done anything like this before. We both waved good-bye to Lisa as I drove away.

We were both silent for a while, listening to the classic rock station on the radio. I wondered what kind of music John liked, or if he even remembered. He just stared out the window with a blank expression on his face that made it hard to tell what he was thinking.

"We just have one stop before we go home," I said. "I have to get my son from school."

He nodded. "I almost forgot you have a kid. Do you think he will have a problem with me staying in the guest house?"

I shook my head. "He helped me get it all ready for you."

A few minutes later, I pulled up at Danny's school. I scanned the playground, looking for him for a few minutes, and then I spotted him. He was on the other side of the yard, and a group of boys who looked much bigger than him were circled around him. They were too far away for me to tell what they were saying, but they seemed to be teasing him about something. One of the boys was right in his face, giving Danny a cold stare. Danny just stood there with his head hanging down. I honked my horn, and he looked up. As soon as he saw me, he ran toward the car. He started to climb into the passenger seat, but when he saw John sitting there, he jumped into the back.

I looked at him and smiled. "Hi, Danny. This is the patient I was telling you about, John. John, this is Danny."

"Hi," they both said at the same time.

I looked at the boys who had been teasing him, and they seemed to scatter to different parts of the playground. "Hey, Danny, were those kids giving you a hard time?"

He looked over at the group of boys. "Who, them? No, we were just fooling around."

I looked at him seriously. "You better be telling me the truth, young man. Because if they're being mean to you, they are going to have to deal with one mad mom."

He laughed. "I'm telling the truth, Mom." Something inside me said that he wasn't being honest, but I didn't want to press him any further in front of John.

"Okay, let's get home; it's been a long day."

CHAPTER

9

When we got home, Danny was excited to show John around. First he gave him the grand tour of our house. He was especially proud of the trophy he had won last year in the national spelling bee. It sat on the mantel, and he had to tell us all about it.

"The word was hypertension," he said. "I remembered it from my mom's medical books. Pretty good for someone who was only in third grade, huh?"

John nodded. "That's really good; you must be pretty smart." He yawned, and I knew that although he was paying attention to everything Danny was saying, he was tired.

"Why don't I show you to the guest house?" I said. "I'm sure you're ready to unwind."

He nodded and followed me through the back door and down the cement path that led to the little guest house.

"Well, here it is. You have the living room here, kitchen right over there, and the bedroom right through here. There's a closet here and another one in the bedroom. There are some extra blankets in the closet, although I doubt you'll need them. I know it's small, but it's all yours for as long as you need it."

He set his bag down, which I knew was full of clothes donated by viewers who had seen his story on the news. People had been very generous, and it made me think that maybe I had been a little too rude to the reporters. If it hadn't been for them, John would really have nothing.

"It's just perfect," he said, looking around in awe. "I really can't thank you enough, Jen. I don't know where I would have gone."

I smiled. "It's no problem, really. I'm just glad this place is finally getting some use. Okay, I will let you get settled in. Just let me know if you need something."

He nodded. "I will."

Later that evening, Danny and I decided to order a pizza for dinner. I wasn't in the mood to cook after such a long day, and pizza was one of Danny's favorite foods, after tacos. After I paid the delivery man, I called Danny in for dinner.

"Pizza, my favorite!" he said as he ran into the kitchen. Then he looked through the window that overlooked the guest house, with a concerned look on his face. "Aren't we going to invite John over for dinner? There isn't much to eat in there, and it's always better to eat with people, don't you think, Mom?"

I nodded. "You're right. You know, I'm proud of you for being so thoughtful. Why don't you go get him?"

John seemed happy to join us for dinner. Although Danny did most of the talking, we had a chance to get to know each other a little better, too. John would start his job at the grocery store next week, and he was happy to have a fresh start. Of course, he still wanted to know who he had been before the accident, but he'd stopped obsessing over it as much. I was glad to see him so relaxed. After dinner, we all had some ice cream for dessert, and Danny challenged him to a game of ping-pong. The ping-pong table had sat in our garage unused for the longest time, and I was glad to see them using it. I joined them for a game myself. I lost, but I was surprised at how much fun it was. After that it was pretty late, so we all said goodnight and went our separate ways. I was relieved that everything was going so well, and happy that I was able to help someone who really needed it.

CHAPTER 10

"Hey, Jen, how's our mystery man doing?" Lisa asked the next morning as I walked up to the nurses' station.

"He's doing really well," I answered. "Danny seems to like him."

"Well, that's good. You know, you really deserve a medal or something for doing this."

I shrugged. "What was I supposed to do, let them throw him out on the street?"

"No, but most people just wait for someone else to do the good deed." I nodded in agreement. "But I'm not most people."

"You've got that right. You're superwoman."

I laughed. "I don't know about that." I grabbed Melissa's file and headed toward her room. When I got there, she was sitting up in her bed with a big smile on her face.

"Good morning, Jen."

"Hi, Melissa. You seem happy today. Much happier than the last time I saw you."

"I got my first baby pictures yesterday." She picked up the ultrasound photos from her bedside table and held them up for me to see. In the center was a tiny, cashew-like baby.

"Awe, what a cutie." I thought about the first time I had seen Danny's little heart fluttering, how magical it was.

Melissa put the picture back down and looked more serious. "I'm really sorry if I got you in trouble with Doctor Martin."

"Don't worry about it." I slid the blood pressure cuff over her arm and looked in her chart to see if there was anything new I should know about.

"You are a great nurse, and I will tell him that if he asks." I could tell by the tone in her voice that she meant it. "And just so you know, I would have decided to keep this baby no matter what you said. Something just tells me it's the right thing to do. This little person is meant to be here."

I nodded. "I just want you to be around, too."

"Well, I plan on it," she said. "You know, there is a doctor in San Francisco, I think his name is Dr. Furguson. He does really cutting-edge surgery to remove tumors like mine, and he specializes in pregnant people. I think he's my best bet. I have been trying to get hold of him, but no luck."

I wondered for a moment why that name sounded familiar, and I thought about Mrs. Furguson. She had told me once that her son was a doctor, and I wondered if that might be him. I was becoming more concerned about her, and I'd thought about trying to contact some family members so she didn't have to spend so much time alone. I wrote Melissa's blood pressure reading in her chart and turned to her with a smile. "If anyone's going to beat this thing, it's going to be you."

The rest of the morning went by quickly. I checked on my patients and organized the supply cabinet. I had always been a bit of a neat freak, so things had to be in order for me to function. Just as I was getting ready to take my lunch break, I got the phone call.

"It's for you, Jen," Lisa said as she handed me the phone.

"Hello?" I was surprised, since I never got phone calls at work.

"Hi," said a man's voice on the other end. "This is Bill Weaver, the principal at Westside elementary school. Is this Jennifer Morrison?"

My heart skipped a beat. Why would the principal be calling me, unless there was a problem with Danny? "Yes, this is she. Is there a problem, sir?"

"I'm afraid there is. Danny got in a fight today. I have a zero-tolerance policy when it comes to this sort of thing, so I have to suspend Danny for the rest of the week. I'm going to need you to come pick him up as soon as possible."

I was in a state of shock as I drove to the school that day. Danny in a fight? He had never been in trouble before, at home or at school. Something just didn't make sense. I thought about the group of boys teasing him the day before, and I wished I had forced Danny to tell me what was going on.

When I arrived at the school office, I saw the boy who had been teasing him. He was big for his age; he must have towered over Danny. He walked past me with a little smirk on his face and disappeared into a classroom across the hall. Then I looked down and saw Danny sitting in a chair, looking down at his feet, clearly ashamed.

"Hi, Danny." I sat down beside him, and he looked up at me. That's when I noticed the black eye, and I gasped, "What happened?"

"Don't worry, Mom. It's not as bad as it looks."

Just then a gray-haired man entered the room. I guessed he was the principal, although he didn't look as I had pictured him.

"Hi, I'm Mr. Weaver," he said, shaking my hand. "Why don't you join me in my office, so we can talk about what happened today?" I nodded and followed him into the small office.

"The kids were in the cafeteria having lunch when the fight broke out," the principal explained. "Danny shoved the other boy, Tommy, and Tommy punched him. The two boys have been having some problems getting along lately, but I'd hoped it would just resolve itself. I'm really hoping that this time away from school will help Danny think about the right way to solve his problems."

I was quiet for a minute while I thought about this. "It just doesn't make sense, sir. Danny's never been a problem child. The other boy must have done something first. I hope he was disciplined as well."

The principal looked down at a paper on his desk, as if he were trying to avoid eye contact. "Don't worry; I took care of it."

I looked at Danny, who was sitting there staring out the window. His eye looked even worse in the light. "Okay, Danny, let's go home," I said.

We were both silent most of the way home. Danny just sat there with the same blank expression on his face. And then, I couldn't take the silence any more.

"I want you to tell me what's going on, son. I know when you aren't being honest with me."

He sighed. "Well, Tommy has been taking my lunch money all year. I finally was fed up, and I didn't want to give it to him. He tried to take it anyway, and that's when I pushed him. Then he socked me right in the eye."

I took a deep breath. "Why didn't you tell anybody?"

He shrugged. "Well, Tommy is Mr. Weaver's nephew. He wouldn't have done anything, anyway. All the teachers are on his side, too. In front of the adults, he acts like a perfect little angel. But behind their backs, he's really mean."

"Well, I'm going to have a talk with his mother."

"Please don't!" Danny cried. "You'll only make him more angry. That's exactly why I didn't tell you. Just let it go."

"I can't let it go," I said. "I don't think it's very fair that you are the one sent home for a week."

"Well, life's not always fair," he said. I thought to myself that he sounded just like me when he said that.

When we got home, I heard hammering coming from out back. Danny and I both walked through the gate to the backyard, curious to see where the sound was coming from. John was standing there, hammering the fence. There was a section of fence that had been broken for years. It had always bothered me, but I'd never taken the time to fix it. When John saw us, he looked up and smiled. I thought to myself how hot he looked. After all, it was nearly one hundred degrees outside. His shirt clung to him, and he wiped the sweat from his brow.

"What ya doing?" Danny asked, walking closer to inspect his work. "Well," he answered, "I noticed the fence needed to be repaired, so I'm fixing it." Then he looked a little closer at Danny's eye. "What happened to you?"

"I got in a fight, and the other guy won."

"I'm sorry to hear that." John took another nail and hammered it into the wood.

"Hey, Danny, why don't you go get started on your homework?" I said. "There's some sliced cheese and crackers you can have for a snack." He nodded and walked into the house. I turned to John, who was grabbing another nail. "Thanks so much for fixing the fence. You didn't have to do that, really."

"I know I didn't. But I wanted to. You're nice enough to let me stay here, and I had to do something to keep busy."

"Well, thanks again," I said. "I was going to grill some chicken for dinner later, if you want to join us."

He smiled. "That sounds perfect."

CHAPTER 11

That evening I worked hard to make sure everything was just right for dinner. I seasoned the chicken to perfection, made a beautiful salad with every vegetable imaginable, and scrubbed the potatoes until my hands were sore. The grill was already hot, and I was just about to put the chicken on when Danny came running into the kitchen.

"Can I cook the chicken tonight?"

I looked down at the plate of raw chicken with a nervous sigh. "Well, I don't know, Danny. You've never really done this by yourself before."

"Don't you think it's time I learned? Come on, Mom, what's the worst thing that could happen?"

"I guess you have a point." I handed him the plate, and he walked over to the grill with a big smile on his face.

I finished tossing the salad and put the potatoes in the oven, trying my best not to hover. One of the hardest parts about being a parent is letting your children grow up. But I knew that Danny could do a lot for himself if I would just give him the chance. I thought about what his father had said; maybe it was partially true. Maybe I babied him too much. When all of the side dishes were finished, I took a peek out the window, and I smiled. John was standing with Danny over the grill, showing him how to turn the chicken. They were both laughing and clearly having a good time. I found myself wishing that his father would spend time with him like that.

"It sure smells good out here," I said as I walked through the sliding glass door that led to the backyard.

Danny beamed. "It's going to be the best chicken you've ever had."

"I'm sure it is." I smiled at John, and he smiled back.

A little while later, we were all sitting around the table, digging into our food. Everything was delicious, and we ate quietly for the longest time. I finally broke the silence.

"So, John, you'll be starting the job at the grocery store next week?"

He nodded. "I can't wait. It will be good to have something to keep me busy, to keep my mind off of the obvious."

I chewed my food and wiped my face with a napkin. "Are the police doing anything to help you figure out who you are?"

"Yes," he said. "They took my fingerprints, and they are trying to match them to the ones they have on file. Of course, I would only have fingerprints on file if I was a criminal or I had a job that required them."

Danny seemed deep in thought for a moment, and then he looked at John with a curious expression. "So, you really can't remember anything from before your accident?"

John shook his head. "Nope. Sometimes I have little flashbacks. When we were grilling the chicken together, I remembered doing that before, but I can't remember when or where—nothing that would help me figure out who I was before."

Danny nodded. "I bet that's hard. I can't imagine forgetting everything."

"It's rough," John answered. "But I get by."

I took a drink of my water and looked at Danny, who was chewing on his chicken leg. "Speaking of things that are rough, we need to figure out what to do with you for the rest of the week. And I really think I should have some words with your principal. I still don't think it's very fair that you're suspended and the other kid gets away with hitting you and taking your lunch money."

John looked shocked. "Someone's been taking his lunch money?"

I nodded. "And the kid is the principal's nephew, so he's getting away with everything."

"Well, that's just not right." John shook his head sadly. "I can tell that Danny's not the type of kid to cause trouble."

"He's not," I said. "But I have to work the rest of the week, and he's suspended from school."

Danny looked up from his plate. "Don't worry about me. My teacher gave me all of my work to do at home. I'll be fine by myself while you are at work."

I took a deep breath. "I'm not sure you're ready to be at home by yourself all day."

Danny looked down, stirring the food around on his plate. He was clearly embarrassed. "I don't need a babysitter, Mom."

"Well, I can stay with him," said John. "I'm here all day anyway."

"Well, I don't want to trouble you." I took another serving of potatoes.

"It's no trouble at all. Danny and I will have a good time, won't we?" Danny nodded in agreement, with a big smile on his face.

"Well, okay," I said. "But you better be on your best behavior."

"I will, Mom."

CHAPTER 12

When I arrived at work the next day, Mrs. Furguson was waiting for me. She had a towel wrapped around her hand, and I could see blood soaking through it.

"Mrs. Furguson, what happened to your hand?" I asked, bending down to take a closer look.

"Well, I was trying to cut some carrots to go in my stew, and I guess I cut my hand instead."

"I see! Well, let's get it all cleaned up."

I took her to the exam room, where I grabbed some antiseptic ointment and a large cloth bandage. Then I slowly removed the towel from her hand. She had a very large cut, but it wasn't very deep, and it looked like most of the bleeding had stopped.

"It doesn't look very deep, so I don't think you need stitches. I'm just going to put some of this ointment and a nice clean bandage on it, okay? It might sting a little." She nodded, and I dabbed some of the ointment on her wound. She flinched a little, and I quickly covered it with the bandage. "Good as new. The bandage should be changed every day. You can come in, and I can do it for you, okay?"

She nodded. "Okay. Thank you." She looked down at her feet, sadly. Just then, I thought of something I had wanted to ask her.

"Mrs. Furguson, didn't you say your son was a doctor in San Francisco?" She nodded. "I'm so proud of him. He does surgeries on people when no other doctor will. High-risk people."

"And when was the last time you saw him?"

She looked down with a puzzled expression. "Well, I don't know. Christmastime, I guess."

I thought it was sad that she hadn't seen her own son in nearly six months. "Do you have any other children?"

Her eyes started to puddle up. "I had a daughter, but she died in a car crash, years ago." She rummaged around in her purse until she found her wallet, and she opened it to reveal a picture of a good-looking young woman in her early twenties. "Her name was Sarah."

"She was beautiful." I didn't know what else to say.

She folded her wallet and put it back in her purse. "It never gets easier, you know? They say it does, but it just doesn't." I could see the tears starting to trickle down her cheek.

I gave her a hug while she softly cried on my shoulder. I held her for a while, before she pulled away and wiped the tears from her eyes.

"Well, there's no good in sitting here feeling sorry for myself, is there?" She patted me on the shoulder. "Besides, I'm sure you have other patients you should be with."

"Well, I want you to promise you'll come in tomorrow for a clean bandage."

She smiled. "I'll be here. Where else do I have to go?"

By the end of the day, I was tired and ready to get home and have a nice relaxing evening. I had already called to check in on Danny and John at my lunch break. Of coarse everything was fine, and they seemed to be having a good time together. They seemed to have an instant connection. I wondered again what John's life had been like before and why nobody had come forward to claim him. After all, he had to have family out there somewhere, didn't he?

When I arrived home, Danny and John were nowhere to be found. I walked through the house, calling for them. There was no answer. I started to panic, thinking to myself that I was probably crazy for leaving Danny with John all day. After all, I barely knew him. Then I heard laughter coming from the backyard, and I walked outside. I didn't see them at first. There was some wood scattered around the yard, along with a hammer and nails. I heard Danny giggle, and I looked up to see a tree house in the large tree at the far end of the yard, complete with a door and windows.

"Danny, are you up there?"

He peeked through the window. "I'm here, Mom! Isn't this great? John and I built it together."

John peeked through the window behind him. "We used some of the old wood that was in the storage shed. I hope you don't mind."

I smiled. "I don't mind at all." Danny had wanted a tree house in that tree for as long as I could remember, but I hadn't known where to begin with a project like that. As a matter of fact, I had bought the wood with the intention of attempting to build one, but I wouldn't have made it nearly as well as John had. Just then, John climbed down the ladder, with a proud smile on his face.

"Well, what do you think?"

"I think it's great," I answered. "I don't know how you finished this in one day."

He winked. "I had a little help. Actually, Danny's really good at this sort of thing. I was just here to guide him along."

I looked up to see Danny happily playing with his action figures in his new tree house.

"Well, thank you so much," I said. "Danny loves it already, I can tell." I noticed that he was sweating. "Can I get you some water?"

"Sure, that would be great."

I went into the house and brought out two glasses of ice water. I was generous with the ice because it was a very hot day, and I was thirsty myself. I sat next to John at the patio table, and handed him his water.

"Thanks," he said. "So, how was work?"

I shrugged. "It was a long day. I'm glad I have a long weekend coming up."

He nodded. "I can't imagine doing what you do. It must be hard dealing with sick people all the time."

"It is. But I can't picture myself doing anything else. I love knowing that I can make a difference."

He took a long drink of his water. "Well, I really admire you. You work hard at your job, and you're raising Danny on your own. That must be rough."

I nodded. "It's hard sometimes, but we get by. It really helps that he's such a great kid."

"Yes, he is. I really enjoyed spending the day with him." I could tell by the tone of his voice that he really meant it.

I set my glass on the table. "I wish his father enjoyed spending time with him. Danny acts like it's a death sentence when he has to go to his dad's house. And I can hardly blame him. David acts like he wants nothing to do with him."

John shook his head sadly. "That's too bad. I can't imagine being that way to my own child. If I had a kid, I would enjoy every moment I spent with him." Then he looked deep in thought for a moment. "Do you mind me asking what happened with you and your ex-husband?"

"I don't mind, but it's kind of a long story." He smiled. "I have all the time in the world."

"Well, I'll give you the short version. Things were great at first, and we always had fun together. I really thought he was the one I would end up spending the rest of my life with. But soon after we got married, David started to become distant. I should have seen the signs sooner. The smell of perfume, the long business weekends. I tried to ignore the gut feeling I had and pretend everything was okay. But I knew deep down it wasn't. He was spending more and more time with Carolyn."

"Carolyn?" he asked.

I nodded. "She was his secretary at work. He works for an electrical company called Power Solutions. Anyway, they started to spend so much time together, I hardly ever saw him. He always had an excuse. I tried to do everything I could to make things work. Danny was probably conceived during a desperate attempt to keep us together." I looked up at Danny, who was decorating his tree house with some drawings he had made, and I sighed. "But it didn't work. David never wanted kids, at least not with me. We divorced when Danny was just a baby. He and Carolyn are happily married now, with two kids. I guess you could say Danny just doesn't fit into his perfect little family."

John took a deep breath. "Wow, what a jerk. I don't know how anyone could be so mean."

I shrugged. "I guess I learned the hard way that not everyone is nice." He thought about that for a moment. "I don't know how I was before the accident, but I can't imagine doing that to someone. Especially someone as kind as you."

I smiled. "Well, thank you. But I have flaws, too."

"Well, if you do, I haven't seen them." He looked at me and smiled.

I think it was right then that I felt a genuine connection with John. I knew that he was going to be a really good friend, and I was glad I had offered to let him stay in the guest house. I thought to myself that it would be good for me and Danny to have him around. Just then, Danny climbed down from the tree house with a big smile on his face.

"The tree house is looking pretty good, if I say so myself."

"Yes it is," I said. "I'm very proud of you for building it." His expression turned more serious. "Hey, Mom?"

"Yes?"

"Are we still going to the wild animal park this weekend?"

"Sure. Why wouldn't we?"

He shrugged. "I don't know. I thought maybe since I was suspended you might say we can't go."

I pulled him onto my lap and hugged him, just as I used to do when he was little. "I know you didn't do anything wrong. It's just a big misunderstanding."

He relaxed a little before he spoke again. "Can John come with us?" I smiled. "If he wants to come, it's okay with me."

We both looked over at John, who was beaming. "I would love to," he told us.

CHAPTER 13

On Saturday morning I woke up with that feeling that someone was watching me. I looked up to see Danny standing there. He was already dressed, his hair was combed, and he had a big smile on his face.

"Good morning, Danny." I rubbed my eyes sleepily.

"Good morning, Mom. I'm all ready to go."

I looked at the clock on my nightstand to see that it was only seven fifteen.

"Well, Danny, the wild animal park doesn't open until ten o clock. Let's have some breakfast and pack a picnic lunch. By then, it should be time to go."

He nodded, looking a little disappointed. "How about I make my world-famous pancakes?"

I smiled. "That sounds delicious."

He bounced down the hallway to the kitchen, and I got up and jumped in the shower. I decided to wear my jean shorts and a blue tank top, since it was going to be another hot day. I put on just enough makeup to make me look awake. When I was finished, I went out to the kitchen. John was there, talking to Danny while he stirred the pancake batter. I sighed as I looked at the mess all over the counter.

When John saw me, he looked up with a smile. "Good morning."

"Good morning." I grabbed a coffee cup out of the cupboard and went over to the coffee pot to pour myself a cup. I looked over at John. "Would you like some?"

He shook his head. "No, thanks. So, Danny tells me he loves to cook."

I nodded. "He always has. We've always cooked together, haven't we, Danny?"

He nodded, not looking up from his pancake batter. "But I won't tell anyone the secret ingredient for my world-famous pancakes."

I smiled and winked at John. I knew that his secret ingredient was cinnamon, but I never let on that I knew.

After we had all eaten breakfast and cleaned up the mess, I packed a picnic lunch for the three of us. I knew the lines for food there would be long, for food that was overpriced and not very good. There was a little picnic area right outside the wild animal park, and it would be the perfect place for a nice picnic lunch. I packed some chicken sandwiches, apples, potato chips, and chocolate chip cookies for dessert. By the time I was finished, it was nine fifteen, and we all loaded into the car and drove away.

When we arrived at the wild animal park, I wasn't surprised to see the huge lines to get in. It was opening weekend, and with only a few weeks left in school, most of the children were bored and looking for something to do. The main attraction was the giant pandas. There were posters of them everywhere. The female had just given birth to a cub, and I guess that was a really big deal, because it had been on the news.

"Mom, do you think we can see the baby panda?" Danny asked as he ran to get in line.

"Maybe," I answered. "We'll just have to see."

He looked up at John with a smile on his face. "I'm glad you could come with us today."

John smiled and playfully ruffled his hair. "I'm glad, too. This place looks like fun."

As soon as we entered the park, Danny ran to the information booth to grab a map. He had always been fascinated with maps. Sometimes he would spend hours in the backyard hiding treasure and drawing maps so he could find it.

"This place is so cool!" he said. "There's a train ride that takes us all around the park. And there are a ton of animal shows! I want to see the monkeys first; they're right over here."

I laughed. "Okay, you lead the way."

We spent most of the morning looking at the different animals. There were monkeys, birds, zebras, elephants, lions, and tigers. Most of them weren't doing anything exciting, but from the reaction of the people watching them, you would have thought they were the most fascinating things in the world. Danny seemed to be having a great time, and John and I could barely keep up with him. By the time we sat down for the tiger show, I was ready to sit and relax a bit after being on my feet all morning. It was hot, probably the hottest day yet, and I finally broke down and bought three large lemonades from the vendor who was walking around selling things. They were overpriced, and most of the ice was melted, but it was still incredibly refreshing, and I took a long drink. Danny drank most of his in one gulp, and soon after that, I noticed him squirming in his seat.

"Mom, I have to go to the bathroom."

I had noticed the restrooms at the bottom of the stairs. "Okay, do you need anyone to go with you?"

He shook his head. "No, I'm fine." He got up and walked down the stairs to the restrooms.

John and I relaxed in our seats. I could tell that he was enjoying himself, although he hadn't said much for most of the morning. He took a drink of his lemonade and looked at me with a smile.

"Thanks again for bringing me along today, and for everything. I really don't know what I would have done."

I smiled. "Well, thanks for spending time with Danny. I can tell he really likes you."

"I like him, too." He looked around at the crowd of people, deep in thought for a moment. "I just wonder if I might have known someone in this crowd. It still drives me crazy that I can't remember anything from before. And the story has been all over the news. How come none of my family has stepped forward? Was I really that bad of a person?"

I shrugged. "From what I know of you, you're a really nice guy. But I only know you now, I didn't know you before. So, still nothing from the police about your fingerprints?"

He shook his head. "Nope. It's like I have no identity. No fingerprints on file, I didn't have any wallet or ID when they found me, and no one seems to know me."

He looked around again with a sad expression on his face, and I felt sorry for him. I said, "Well, I may not know you very well, but I hope you consider me a friend. And Danny, too."

He nodded, and a slight smile came across his face. "Of course. You two are the only friends I have right now."

For the rest of the afternoon, we all had a great time. We had a nice picnic lunch, and the picnic area wasn't even that crowded. I laughed at the thought of people standing in those long lines in the heat waiting for food, while we sat in the shade enjoying our lunch. We saw a few more shows, and we were there when they brought out the baby panda. Danny was thrilled that we were the first people to see her. At the end of the day, we were all tired and overheated as we left the wild animal park.

* * * *

That night, I went into Danny's room to say goodnight. He was reading a book about animals that we'd purchased earlier at the gift shop.

"I had a really great time today, Mom," he said.

I smiled. "Me too."

He looked down at his book, and then back up at me with a serious expression. "Hey, Mom?"

"Yes, son?"

"I really like John. I'm glad he's staying here for a while." I nodded. "Me too."

CHAPTER 14

Monday morning came before we knew it, and it was a busy day for all of us. Danny was back at school, I had to work, and it was John's first day on the job at the grocery outlet. I told John I would drop him off at work, since it was on the way to Danny's school anyway. I had a pot of coffee brewing and three different types of cereal out for breakfast. I looked at the clock and I was pleased to see we were ahead of schedule. I turned on the morning news, poured myself a cup of coffee, and sat at the table enjoying the peace and quiet.

"Mom!" Danny screamed as he darted into the kitchen.

"What is it, son?"

"Have you seen my green shirt?"

"Which one?"

He sighed in an irritated sort of way. "You know, the one we wear on school spirit day?"

"I think it's in the wash."

Danny didn't look pleased. "But everyone else will be wearing theirs."

I shrugged. "Just tell them you have the worst mother in the world, and she forgot to do the laundry."

"Very funny, Mom," he said as he stomped out of the room.

I laughed a little as I sipped my coffee. Just moments later, John was at the door, and I went to let him in.

"Good morning. Are you all ready for your first day at work?"

"As ready as I'll ever be," he smiled, and I noticed he looked nice in his black slacks and collared shirt. He smelled good, too, although I couldn't place the scent.

"We have some different cereals for breakfast," I said. "I wasn't sure what kind you like."

He shrugged. "I'm really not picky."

Just then, something on the news caught our eyes. A picture of John flashed on the TV screen. It must have been taken while he was in the hospital. Then it went back to the newsroom, where the anchor spoke. She was the same perky blonde I had seen on the station before.

"Sources tell us the mystery man, John Doe, is now residing with his nurse, Jennifer Morrison. He was released from the hospital last week, with a clean bill of health. Here is more from one of the doctors who was treating him at Sacramento Grace."

Doctor Martin appeared on the screen. He was standing outside the hospital with a serious expression. "John Doe came to us a little over a week ago, with a mild concussion. After we assessed the patient, we realized he had no memory from before the accident. This type of amnesia is usually just temporary, and we have reason to hope that eventually he will regain his memory. Unfortunately, with no type of identification in the vehicle or on Mr. Doe himself, there is no way to identify who he is. We do know that he is in excellent health, and we were glad that we could be a part of his speedy recovery."

John laughed. "Like he really cares about anyone but himself. That guy is such a jerk."

I nodded. "Try working with him."

John's picture flashed on the screen again, with the voice of the anchor in the background. "If you know this man, please call the number on the screen." The number flashed on the screen, and it went back to the newsroom, where the anchor was now sitting with an older, gray-haired gentleman.

"That is such an interesting story," he said cheerfully.

The anchorwoman nodded in agreement. "Yes, it is. More people should be like the nurse who took him in. Of course, she might have her own reasons for doing that."

The gray-haired man smiled a mischievous grin. "Like what?"

"Like maybe there's something more going on than a patient-nurse relationship. She's a single mom; he doesn't remember anything. I'm just saying, it's a possibility." They both laughed before they went on to the next story, and John and I stood there in stunned silence.

I turned the TV off and looked over at John. "That's just ridiculous. I swear that station will do anything to boost their ratings."

He nodded in agreement. "Yeah, I can't believe them."

Just then, Danny came back into the kitchen, wearing a plain green shirt that was at least two sizes too small for him. He clearly wasn't pleased about it, and he stormed over to the table to sit down.

"Okay, let's eat," I said. "We all have a busy day ahead of us."

We were all quiet as we ate breakfast and during the drive to the grocery outlet. Danny was still fuming about his green shirt, and I kept thinking about what the news anchor had said. I was sure John was thinking the same thing. When I pulled up in front of the store, I was pleased to see John had ten more minutes before his shift started.

"Well, here you are," I said. "Good luck."

"Thanks," he said. "And don't worry; I haven't forgotten what I said before. As soon as I get my first paycheck, I'm going to pay you rent."

I shrugged. "No rush. Call me if you need a ride home later."

"I will." He looked at Danny, who was sitting in the back seat with his arms crossed over his chest. "Have a good day at school, little buddy."

Danny nodded, with the same sullen look on his face. "I'll try."

We both waved to John as he disappeared into the store, and I drove off. When I pulled up in front of Danny's school just a short while later, cars and children were everywhere, as usual. It was always crazy in the mornings, and it reminded me how nice it would be when school was over for summer break. I looked at Danny, who still had that depressed expression across his face.

"I'm sorry about your shirt," I said sympathetically. "I'll make sure it's clean next week."

"Okay." He grabbed his backpack and got out of the car, running toward his classroom.

"Hey, Danny," I called after him.

He turned around to face me. "What?"

"I love you."

He smiled the faintest little smile. "Love you too, Mom."

I watched as he walked toward the school and disappeared into his classroom. Then something else caught my eye. I saw the boy who had been teasing Danny, the one who had given him the black eye. Tommy. His mother was walking with him to the classroom. I watched as Tommy entered the classroom, and his mother started to walk away. I quickly got out of my car and walked over to her. I had some words for her. Nobody bullied my son.

"Excuse me!" I called. At first, she kept on walking, but when she realized it was directed to her, she turned around, looking at me with a puzzled expression. "I'm Jennifer Morrison, Danny's mom."

Her face registered recognition. "Yes, I've seen Danny around. Is there a problem?"

I nodded. "Yes, there is. Your son has been teasing Danny and taking his lunch money. Last week, he hit him and gave him a black eye. Danny was suspended because he pushed him, but I really just think he was trying to defend himself."

She looked honestly shocked, as if she'd known nothing about this. "I'm so sorry! I'll talk to him tonight, I promise." It was then that I noticed the tears start to well up in her eyes, and before I knew it, she was sobbing. She tried frantically to wipe the tears away as fast as they came.

"It's okay, really," I said. "I just wanted you to know what was happening, so you could talk to Tommy."

She shook her head. "No, it's not that. You see, his father died just a few months back. Actually, he committed suicide. He shot himself, and Tommy was the one who found him. I thought Tommy was adjusting well, but now I just don't know. To top it all off, I just lost my job, which means we just lost our medical insurance, and Tommy has severe asthma. I have no idea how I'm going to pay for his medication. I can't do this all on my own." She started crying harder now, and I just stood there in stunned silence, not knowing what to do. So I gave her a hug.

"I had no idea," I said quietly.

"Well, how could you know?" she said through her tears. "It's not exactly something I like to talk about."

I nodded. "Well, I'm very sorry for your loss."

"Thank you. And I promise I will talk to Tommy tonight. He may have been through a lot recently, but it doesn't make it okay for him to hurt someone."

We went our separate ways, and I was amazed at how different Tommy's mom was from the way I had imagined her. It reminded me how important it is not to judge people. It also made me thankful that at least Danny had his father in his life. That was more than Tommy would ever have. I had gone into that conversation expecting something totally different. But then again, as I had learned from my own experience, life rarely goes as planned.

CHAPTER 15

A short while later, while I was at work, I still couldn't stop thinking about my conversation with Tommy's mom. I couldn't imagine what she was going through—and what Tommy was going through, for that matter. It just broke my heart to think about it. I went about my day, checking on my patients, but a part of me was still at the school.

My first stop was Melissa's room. When I got there, she was sound asleep, and she didn't look very good. She was so pale, and her breathing was shallow. I took her temperature and blood pressure, but she just slept through most of it, barely opening her eyes. I went back out to the nurses' station, where Lisa was doing some paperwork.

"Have you been in to see Melissa this morning?" I asked. "She doesn't look so good."

She nodded. "She's suddenly taken a turn for the worse. And the crazy part is, she was doing better over the weekend. They were about to let her go home, and she was really excited." She looked down, shaking her head sadly. "The doctors are saying that if her tumors grow any more, she will be paralyzed."

I took a deep breath. "Paralyzed? But Melissa's such a fighter. There's got to be something they can do!"

Lisa just shrugged. "Well, there's surgery, but none of the surgeons here will do it, because she's pregnant and it makes it more risky."

Just then, Melissa's husband, Jack, came up to the nurses' station. He looked tired, as if he hadn't been getting much sleep. And how could he, with his wife so sick?

"Hi, Jack," I said. "Here to see Melissa?"

He nodded. "We were hoping she'd be home by now. How's she doing today?"

"Well, she was sleeping when I went to check on her, but I'm sure she'll be glad to see you." I smiled, but he didn't smile back. He just rubbed his eyes and yawned. Then he looked at me with tears in his eyes.

"There's got to be something somebody can do for her. She is the most amazing person I've ever met, and I can't imagine my life without her. The doctors say it's only a matter of time before she's paralyzed, or dead. I just can't accept that." The tears started streaming down his face. My heart really went out to him, but I had no idea what to do. He finally wiped his tears away and walked silently to Melissa's room; the door closed loudly behind him.

Shortly after that, Mrs. Furguson arrived to have her bandage changed. I was relieved to have such a simple task after such an emotionally draining morning.

"Hello, Mrs. Furguson. How are you today?"

She looked up at me with sad eyes. "I'm feeling old today. This morning, I fell in the shower and couldn't get up."

I gasped. "Are you okay?"

She nodded. "Besides this bruise, I'm all right." She lifted her shirt to reveal a huge bruise that covered most of her right side.

"That had to hurt."

"It did. I think I fell so hard I left a dent." She laughed a nervous little laugh, but I didn't think it was very funny.

"Hey, Mrs. Furguson, is there anyone close by who could come and help you out sometimes? Like a neighbor or relative?"

She shook her head. "Not really. My siblings have all passed away, my neighbors all work, and all of my other family members are scattered all over the country."

I nodded, thinking how sad it must feel to be so alone. No wonder she was coming to the hospital all the time. We were probably her only friends.

The rest of the day went by pretty quickly, and before I knew it, it was time to go home. I picked up Danny from his after-school program, and we stopped by the store for a few groceries. I was in the mood for a good steak, and I grabbed an extra one for John. He hadn't called me to come get him yet, so I assumed he had found a ride home. And I was right, because when we got home, he was sitting out back at the patio table, drinking a beer.

"Hey, John!" Danny said as he ran outside to greet him.

John looked up with a smile. "Hey, little buddy, how was your day?" Danny shrugged. "It was okay. I didn't get in a fight or get suspended, so I guess that's a good thing."

John laughed. "Yes, it is."

Danny ran off to play in his tree house, and I sat next to John at the patio table. "How was your first day at work?"

"It went really well," he answered. "No complaints. One of my co-workers gave me a ride home, and he said we can carpool to work, since we have the same shift."

I nodded. "That's good, but it really isn't a problem to take you."

"I know," he said. "But you've done enough for me already. Anyway, I haven't asked how your day was."

"Well, it was draining," I said. "I'll tell you all about it later, but right now, that beer sure looks good."

He smiled. "One cold one coming up."

That night John grilled the steaks, and I made some vegetables and rice to go with them. We all ate outside at the patio table. We were laughing and talking, enjoying our meal, when the phone rang.

"I'll get it!" Danny said as he ran into the house to grab the phone.

John looked up and wiped his face with a napkin. "So, why was your day so draining, anyway? I mean, I know you have a high-stress job, but did something happen today with one of your patients?"

I nodded. "Well, a couple of them, but it all started at Danny's school this morning. I saw Tommy's mom. He's the boy who gave Danny the black eye. It turns out his father committed suicide a few months ago, and Tommy found him."

John gasped. "I can't imagine! No wonder the kid's so messed up."

I took another serving of rice, and I sighed. "I feel sorry for his mom, too."

Just then Danny came back out, with the phone to his ear. "Yes, Grandma, she's right here. Okay, bye." He held out the phone, and I took a deep breath. I loved my mom dearly, but I was glad she lived so far away. She had this habit of snooping into other people's business, and most of the time she still treated me like a child. And I hadn't told her about John yet, so I knew she would have some words about that. I took the phone and held it up to my ear.

"Hi, Mom."

"Hi, Jen." Just with those few words, I could sense her disapproval. "So, what's this I hear about some man staying in your guest house?"

Oh boy, I thought, *here we go*. "He was a patient of mine who needed a place to stay," I told her. "So he's staying in the guest house for a while until he figures things out."

"Uh huh," she said with a sigh. "Well, what do you know about this man? Is he really someone who should be around my grandson?"

"He's a nice guy, Mom. Danny really likes him."

"Well, nice guys can be serial killers, or rapists," she said. "It happens all the time."

I tried to cut a piece of my steak while balancing the phone with my shoulder. "Would you please be a little more optimistic? I'm a very good judge of character."

"Oh, really?" I knew what she was going to say before the rest of the words left her mouth. "What about Danny's father? You weren't such a good judge of character then, were you?"

I silently chewed my steak for a moment, not wanting to answer, and she took the cue and continued.

"Well, the reason I'm calling is because your father and I are flying down next Tuesday. I was hoping we could stay in the guest house, but it sounds like it's occupied."

I rolled my eyes. "Don't worry, Mom; we'll make room for you."

Later that night, after Danny was in bed, I couldn't stop thinking about everything that had happened that day. I wondered what I could do to help everyone: Melissa, Mrs. Furguson, Tommy, and his mom. I knew I couldn't help everyone at once, but I had to start somewhere. I went to my computer, and in the search engine I typed "Dr. Furguson in San Francisco."

Immediately a website popped up with a picture of a middle-aged man. His eyes looked just like Mrs. Ferguson's, so I knew I had the right guy. It was a medical website, with links for all sorts of medical problems. Over his photo, it said, "Dr. Richard Furguson, award-winning surgeon in the Bay area." There was a link to a newspaper article about him, and I clicked on it. There was another picture of him, and an article with the title, "Miracle Doctor Saves a Cancer Patient and Her Unborn Baby." Excited, I read on.

Some are calling him the miracle doctor, but to Doctor Richard Furguson, it's just another day on the job. He recently preformed a twelve-hour surgery on patient Lilly Thompson, who was in her seventh month of pregnancy. She had already been turned down by a dozen other surgeons, who refused to perform the surgery during her pregnancy. Lilly had several massive tumors on her spine. If she had waited until she delivered, the outcome might not have been a happy one for her or the baby. But thanks to the amazing hands of Doctor Furguson, little Connor is doing just fine.

"He's such a miracle," gushes the proud mother as she cradles her son. "No words can describe how grateful I am to Dr. Furguson for giving both of us the miracle of life."

I knew that if Melissa and her baby were going to have a chance, Doctor Furguson was the best bet. I went back to his web page and scribbled down his phone number and the address of his office in San Francisco. Then I rubbed my eyes and realized how tired I was. It had been a long day. I slowly walked down the hallway to my room, and as soon as my head hit the pillow, I was asleep.

CHAPTER 16

The next morning I stopped in at the cafeteria for a coffee. Mac greeted me cheerfully, even though he was flipping pancakes, pouring orange juice, and taking someone's order all at the same time. He had always been really good at multitasking.

"Hi, Jen. Your usual, right? Or are you feeling a little adventurous today?"

I laughed. "I'll have the usual today. Maybe sometime soon I'll work up the nerve to try something new. Then you won't know what to do with me." He smiled and handed a plate of pancakes to a customer. Then he went to make my drink. I looked around and noticed how busy it was today. Almost every table was filled with people, and the sound of conversation filled the room. Then I noticed Melissa's husband, Jack. He was sitting at a back table sipping his coffee. A bagel sat on the table before him, but it was untouched. The bags under his eyes were obvious. It looked as if he hadn't slept at all.

"Here's your drink, Jen," Mac called. I reached into my purse and pulled out the money. He handed me the drink.

"Thanks, Mac."

"No problem."

I sipped my drink and walked over to the table where Jack was sitting. "Hi, Jack."

He looked up at me. "Oh, hi. How are you?"

"I'm fine, but you don't look like you are. Why don't you go home and get some rest? Melissa will be in good hands today."

"I know she will," he sighed, and he took a drink of his coffee. "I just keep thinking, each time I see her, that it might be the last. I hate to think that way, and don't ever tell her I told you this, but I'm starting to lose hope. There's a small part of me that wishes she'd just ended the pregnancy. Then at least I'd still have her."

I sat down across from him. "I think there's a way you can have both Melissa and the baby. There's a doctor in San Francisco; his name is Doctor Furguson."

He held up his hand. "I've heard all about good old Doctor Furguson. He's supposed to be a miracle surgeon, right? He did surgery on some pregnant woman when no one else would?"

I nodded. "Yes, he's supposed to be the best."

"Well, then how come he never returns phone calls? Melissa and I have tried to call him at least a dozen times, and he has yet to call back. Meanwhile, I have to sit and watch my wife get sicker and sicker all the time because the medication that could shrink her tumors isn't safe during pregnancy. Last night, I was up with her half the night while she screamed in agony. And Melissa's not a complainer, you know that. It breaks my heart that I can't do anything to help her." I could see the tears starting to trickle down his cheek.

I patted him on the shoulder. "If anyone can get through this, it's Melissa. I promise I will do whatever I can to help make sure both she and the baby make it out of this all right."

He sighed an irritated sigh and stood up, preparing to leave. "Don't make promises you can't keep, okay?"

"I'm not. And one more thing before you go."

"What?"

"She's lucky to have you for her husband. I can tell you really love her." He smiled a faint little smile. "Thanks." Then he walked away.

Later that day, when I was on my lunch break, I got my purse and pulled out the piece of paper with Doctor Furguson's number on it. I dialed the number on my cell phone, and I wasn't surprised when it rang three times and then went over to his voice mail. "Hello, you've reached Doctor Richard Furguson. I can't get to the phone right now, but if you leave a message with your name and number, I will get back to you. *Beep*."

I took a deep breath before I spoke. "Hello, my name is Jennifer Morrison; I'm a nurse at Sacramento Grace Hospital. I've read about some of the wonderful work you have done, and I have a patient who might benefit from your services. Please call me at 5-3-8, 6-7-6-5. Thank you." I sighed as I closed the phone. I had a feeling he wasn't going to call me back, but it was worth a shot.

When Danny and I arrived home later that evening, the smell of food cooking was coming from the backyard. We went through the gate and to the backyard, where John was standing over the grill. When he saw us, he looked up and smiled.

"Hi. Hope everyone's hungry. I did a little shopping after work. I've got hamburgers and hot dogs. There's potato and macaroni salad, too."

I smiled. "We're starved."

A short while later, we were all sitting around the patio table, laughing and talking as we ate. I was beginning to really like having John around, and I could tell Danny felt the same way. John talked about his day at work and how the grocery store was becoming busier as the summer months approached. And Danny told us about his day at school. I wasn't surprised when he said that Tommy hadn't tried to take his lunch money.

"He apologized for being so mean to me before, and he wants to be friends now. He wants me to come to his birthday party."

"Well, I'm glad you two are getting along now," I said with a smile, and John nodded in agreement.

After dinner, we cleaned up our mess, which consisted of throwing our paper plates away and putting some containers in the fridge. John and Danny went to finish decorating the tree house, and I went to the other room to make a phone call. I tried to call Doctor Furguson's number again. Of course, nobody answered. This time I didn't bother to leave a message. I had already decided what I was going to do. If he wasn't going to answer his phone, then I would go to San Francisco and find him myself.

CHAPTER 17

That weekend was Danny's weekend with his father. As always, he wasn't very happy about that, and he let me know it.

"I don't want to go," he complained. "Megan has a dance recital, and it's gonna be *so* boring! I'd rather stay here and read my book or play in my new tree house."

"I know you would," I said. "But sometimes you have to do things you don't want to do. I know your dad isn't exactly your favorite person, but at least he's around for you to spend time with. Some people aren't so lucky, you know."

He rolled his eyes. "Yeah, I feel really lucky."

I put some extra clothes in his bag and made a mental note to wash his green shirt before Monday. "You should feel lucky. You know, Tommy doesn't have a dad anymore."

His eyes widened; he was clearly surprised to hear that. "He doesn't?"

"Nope."

"What happened?"

"He died." I didn't want to go any further into detail.

He was quiet, considering that for a moment. "Well, I don't want him to die or anything. Maybe I could just see him, like, once a year. And maybe you could marry John; then he could be my dad."

I stood in stunned silence, not knowing what to say, but the silence was broken when the doorbell rang. Danny grabbed his bag and ran toward the door. I followed him, trying my best to keep up. He opened the door to see David standing there, with an impatient expression on his face.

"Come on Danny, let's go."

"Wait a minute," I said, looking at Danny. "Can I have a hug first?" Danny smiled his crooked little smile and ran into my arms, hugging me tight. "Love you, Mom."

"Love you, too. Have a good weekend."

David rolled his eyes, clearly annoyed with our display of affection. "Can we go now?"

Danny nodded, and he followed him out to the car. I watched as he got in and drove away.

Later that night, I got on my computer and googled directions to Doctor Furguson's office. I printed it out and put it in an envelope, along with Melissa's x-rays. I would probably get in trouble for taking them, but I didn't care. I had my patient's best interest at heart, and that was all that mattered. My thoughts were interrupted when there was a knock at the back door. I knew it had to be John, because no one else ever came through the back door. When I opened the door, I saw John standing there, holding a tub of French vanilla ice cream in one hand and an apple pie in the other.

"I thought maybe you might like some dessert," he said, smiling.

I nodded. "I would love some," I said, and I let him in.

He cut us each a piece of pie and scooped some ice cream to go with it.

We sat on the couch together, eating quietly, enjoying the moment.

"Thanks for this," I said. "How did you know apple pie is my favorite?" He laughed. "I didn't; it was on sale. And I get a discount at the grocery store, so it really was almost free." He took another bite, deep in thought for a moment. "So, Danny is with his dad this weekend?"

I nodded. "Yep. Every other weekend. He hates it, but I do think it's important for him to at least see his father."

He wiped his face with a napkin before he spoke again. "Do you have any plans for the weekend?"

I nodded. "I'm going to San Francisco tomorrow. There is a surgeon there, and I think he might be able to help one of my patients. Well, two of them, really. One needs life-saving surgery, the other one is his mother. She doesn't need surgery; she just needs him to spend a little more time with her."

He nodded. "Well, I think you're a great nurse. I can tell you really care about your patients."

"I do." I took another bite of my pie. "Hey, John, why don't you come with me?"

"To San Francisco?"

"Sure, why not? We can make a day of it. I can show you around the city, and we can eat in one of those restaurants that overlook the bay. It will be fun."

He scratched his head, thinking it over for a minute. "Well, I do have the day off, and if I've been to San Francisco, I can't remember. So, sure. I'd love to!"

CHAPTER

18

The next morning I got up extra early and took a shower. I had a hard time deciding what to wear, since I knew it would be a bit cooler in the Bay area. I finally decided to wear tan shorts and a white short-sleeved shirt, and I packed a sweatshirt and a pair of long pants, just in case. Then I went downstairs, where the coffee pot was full of hot coffee. I poured myself a cup and sat down at the table, sipping it slowly.

Just a few minutes later, John showed up at the back door. He looked as if he had just showered, too, because his hair was still damp. The green shirt he was wearing really brought out the color in his eyes, and I noticed he was holding a brown grocery bag.

"I thought I'd bring a few snacks for the road," he said with a smile. "Have you ever had SunChips?"

I nodded. "I love them. They're my favorite, besides Cheetos." He pulled out a bag of Cheetos. "I have those, too."

"Well, you're my new best friend, then," I joked. "Are you ready to hit the road?"

He nodded. "As ready as I'll ever be."

The drive to the Bay area was congested, as usual, with the normal traffic jams. John and I were pretty quiet for most of the drive there, munching on some cereal bars as I drove. We stopped at a rest stop along the way, to use the bathroom and stretch our legs. Even the rest stop was busy. There was a line to use the bathroom, and every picnic table was filled with people. They were mostly young families, trying to let their children get their wiggles out. I saw one boy about Danny's age playing catch with his dad, and I thought of him. I knew he would probably be having much more fun with John and me. San Francisco was one of his very favorite places. But I knew that soon he would be out of school for the whole summer. I would make another trip with him then. Right now, I was on a mission. I had some words to say to Doctor Furguson. John and I got back in the car and continued our drive. This time the traffic jams seemed to let up, and it was smooth sailing the rest of the way there.

As we crossed the Golden Gate Bridge, John's eyes widened. He had a look of wonder on his face that reminded me of a child seeing something for the very first time. I continued to drive into the city, and as I got closer to Doctor Furguson's office, I pulled out my map and asked John to help navigate.

"Okay, we are looking for 2351 Clay Street," he said matter-of-factly. "It should be coming up about half a mile from here." I continued to drive, watching the street signs closely. Finally, we arrived at our destination. It was a small medical building that was shared by a few doctors. I pulled up into the small parking lot to the side. There was a large sign that said Patient Parking Only. I knew we wouldn't be there long.

I turned to John. "Okay, this looks like the place. Do you want to come in with me?"

He shook his head. "I'll just wait here. I've got some magazines I can read."

I nodded and grabbed the envelope that contained Melissa's x-rays. When I entered the building, there was a large desk where a dark-haired woman sat, talking on the phone. When she saw me, she gestured that it would be just a minute. I looked around. It was a nice-looking medical office. All of the furniture looked new. There were a few patients waiting, sitting quietly reading magazines. Finally, the woman got off the phone.

"Can I help you?"

I looked at her and smiled. "I'm here to see Doctor Furguson."

"Do you have an appointment?"

"Well, no. I've been trying to call him, but he hasn't returned my calls. I'm a nurse in Sacramento, and I think one of my patients could really benefit from his services."

She nodded in a sympathetic way. "I see. Well, he's all booked up for the rest of the week. I can make an appointment for you, if you'd like."

I sighed. "I didn't drive all the way here to be turned away, and my patient really doesn't have much time. I won't take much of his time, I promise. But I'm not leaving until I speak with him." I crossed my arms over my chest in a stubborn way, and she looked surprised that I wasn't giving up so easily.

"I'll go tell him you're here," she said quietly, and she walked through the back door to the office that was labeled Dr. Richard Furguson. Just seconds later, she emerged with a smile on her face. "He will see you now. Just make it quick, he has a full load of patients today."

I nodded and went through the doors and into his office. He was sitting at his desk, typing something on his computer. He looked much older than he did in the picture on his website, but the resemblance between him and his mother was amazing. When he heard me enter, he looked up and sighed.

"You must be Jennifer, right?"

"Yes. I'm a nurse at Sacramento Grace."

"And how can I help you?"

I cleared my throat nervously. "Well, sir, I have a patient who I think you might be able to help. Her name is Melissa, and she has several tumors on her spine, as well as in her brain. She's also about eight weeks pregnant. I've been reading about some of the work you've done, and I must say I was very impressed. I think you are the right surgeon to do the job." I took Melissa's x-rays out of the envelope and spread them out on his desk. He looked them over for a few minutes, and he shook his head.

"You were reading about my work on Lilly Thompson, right?"

I nodded. "She was pregnant, too, and you were able to save her and the baby. Melissa wants nothing more than to be a mother, and I think—"

He held up his hand to cut me off. "Well, first of all, Lilly's tumors weren't nearly this big. And this patient's tumors are in more risky spots. I'm sorry, there's nothing I can do." He handed me the x-rays and turned back to his computer.

"Her name is Melissa."

He looked up from the computer. "What?"

"Her name is Melissa, sir."

"Well, whatever her name is, I really don't think I can help her. Now, if you don't mind, I have other patients to see."

I started to walk away, with my head hanging down. But then I stopped dead in my tracks and turned back to face him. "There's one more thing."

He sighed in an irritated way. "What's that?"

"I've also been treating your mother, Ann Furguson." He nodded. "What about her?"

"Well, quite frankly, I'm worried about her. She seems to be getting more confused lately. I don't think she's always remembering to eat. And, just the other day, she fell in the shower."

"And why are you telling me this?"

"Well, she's your mother. I thought maybe you could help her out sometimes."

He looked at me with a frown. "Listen, if I had more time to spend with her, I would. I have a full patient load, and my teenage son has been in and out of trouble for a while now. So if it's really getting that bad, to the point where she can't take care of herself, then maybe it's time to put her in a home."

I shivered at the thought of Mrs. Furguson in a nursing home. I had always thought they were horrible places where old people went to die.

"Well, I don't think she needs to go to a home," I said quietly. "She just needs more time with her family."

"Well, like I said, if I had more time, I would."

"I hope you find some time, soon. You're the only child she has left." Those words seemed to enrage him, and at first I didn't understand why.

"What has she told you about Sarah?" he demanded.

I shrugged. "Just that she died in a car crash many years ago."

He put his head in his hand, and shook his head. "Did she tell you I was driving the car?"

"No, she didn't mention that."

"Of course not. Because deep down, she still blames me."

I could tell he had more to say, and I sat down in the chair across from him before he continued.

"I was driving her to a Christmas party. She didn't want to go; she'd had some kind of falling out with the people who were throwing it. But I didn't want to go alone, so I convinced her to come with me." He paused for a minute, trying to compose himself. "A dog ran into the road, and I swerved to try to avoid it. We headed right into oncoming traffic, and another car hit us dead on. She died instantly." I could see tears in his eyes, but he quickly wiped them away. "Sarah was my mother's world; they did everything together. So I don't blame her for not forgiving me. I don't forgive myself. Now, like I said, I have patients I need to see. I wish I could help your patient, but I just can't. And I wish I had more time to spend with Mom, but I don't. And even if I did, I just can't face her."

I quietly got up and walked to the door. Before I left, I had one more thing I wanted to say. "Your mother told me she's proud of you. She loves you, and I know she would be happy to see you. I know that, because when she talks about you, I hear nothing but love in her voice." With that, I turned around and walked out the door, not looking back.

CHAPTER

19

When I got back to the car, John was sitting quietly, looking at the newest edition of Us Magazine. I got in the drivers seat, pounded my fists against the steering wheel, and screamed.

He dropped his magazine and looked at me with a shocked expression. "I guess that didn't go the way you hoped it would."

"No, it didn't. He doesn't even want to try to help Melissa. And he thinks the best solution for his mom is to put her in a home! He won't even try to talk to her about the real issue going on between them. It's so frustrating!" I took some deep breaths to calm myself down. "Let's get out of here," I said. I put the key into the ignition, started the car, and drove away.

A short while later I pulled up to Fisherman's Wharf. I figured since John had no memories of San Francisco it was a good place to start. He looked around with wonder at all the people.

"Wow, this place is really something."

I smiled. "Yes, it is. This is Danny's favorite spot. He would probably kill me if he knew we were here without him. I feel like a bad mom coming here with you while he has to spend the weekend at his dad's house."

He shook his head. "You're a great mom; he's lucky to have you." After a pause, he looked at me, curious. "Hey, Jen?"

"What?"

"Did you ever think about having more children? I mean, I just think you're so good at it."

I sighed. "Well, I've thought about it, sure. But after I had Danny, I was told I had premature ovarian failure. That means my baby-making factory shut down early. I feel lucky to have him, though."

John nodded, and we didn't say anything more after that.

After I found a parking spot, we spent some time walking along Pier 39. We watched the sea lions for a while, and then we looked through the telescopes they had set up. I showed Alcatraz and Angel Island to John. He seemed in awe as he took in all of the sights and sounds of the city. After we had spent some time walking around, we were ready for lunch. We both got a bread bowl of clam chowder, and we sat on a dock overlooking the bay. It was surprisingly warm for the Bay area, but still much cooler than Sacramento. We ate quietly, enjoying the moment. I hadn't realized how hungry I was, and before I knew it, I had eaten every last bite.

John finished up and threw his leftovers into a nearby garbage can. "That was amazing food!"

I nodded in agreement. "The company is pretty nice, too. Thanks for coming with me today."

He smiled. "There's no place I'd rather be."

We walked around for a while longer, and then we made our way down to the information area to get some tickets for a ferry ride. I figured that after the ferry ride we could get some dinner and then head home. I knew that if we left too late, traffic would be worse.

John and I sat next to each other as the ferry circled Angel Island and Alcatraz. The cool breeze of the bay felt incredibly refreshing after the heat wave we'd had lately. We listened as the recorded message on the overhead speaker told us the history of both islands. John looked very interested, but I had heard the same thing at least twenty times. I could probably recite it by heart.

At one point, the ferry made a turn that pushed John and me closer together. We both laughed at first, but then we were staring into each other's eyes. For a minute, I thought he might kiss me, but then the ferry pulled into its station, and the voice coming from the loudspeaker announced it was time to exit. I thought to myself that it was crazy to think there might be something romantic between us. He didn't even know who he was. What if he had a wife somewhere out there? Or kids? And I pushed those thoughts out of my mind, as we walked along the bay and then to the Bubba Gump restaurant for dinner.

John was quiet during dinner; I could tell he was thinking about something. We ordered our food; John chose the fish and chips and I opted for the bucket of shrimp.

"Penny for your thoughts," I said, taking a long drink of water.

"Oh, I'm just thinking that I'm having a great time with you today." He spread his napkin on his lap and looked at me with a smile. "But I'm confused about something."

"What's that?"

"Why on earth did your ex-husband let you go? I mean, if you were mine, I could never do that. I would show you every day for the rest of my life how special you are."

My stomach did somersaults at the sound of his words. It wasn't so much what he'd said, it was the way he'd said it. I could tell he was totally sincere. We stared silently into each other's eyes, until the waitress broke the silence when she brought out our food.

John and I were quiet, for the most part, as we ate our dinner and during the ride home. It was as if we were both trying to avoid talking about what was on our minds, even though we both knew perfectly well what that was. There were feelings between us, that was for certain. But what to do about those feelings was another story. It was complicated. I didn't know whether there was a way to make it work between us, even if we wanted to.

The traffic wasn't nearly as bad as it had been on the way to the city. There was a steady flow all the way home. When I pulled up in front of the house that evening, it was just starting to get dark. I was happy we'd made such great timing.

"Well, here we are," I said as I pulled the keys out of the ignition. "I had a really great time today."

He nodded. "Me too."

I remember what happened next as if it were yesterday. He leaned over, pulled me toward him, and kissed me—slowly at first, but quickly becoming more urgent. It had been a long time since I'd kissed a man, and the feel of his lips against mine was incredible. I kissed him back, but then the sensible side of me took over, and I pulled away.

"We can't do this."

"Why not?"

I took a deep breath, trying to calm myself down. I realized my heart was practically beating out of my chest. "There are at least a hundred reasons why not. For one thing, I promised myself that I wouldn't take any relationship lightly. Not just for me, but Danny—"

He held up his hand to cut me off. "I like Danny and he likes me. I don't think he would have a problem with it. And this isn't something *I* take lightly, either. I've given it a lot of thought. What else?"

"Well," I continued. "It goes against the patient-nurse relationship. And you don't even know where you came from. What if you already have a wife, or kids?"

He shook his head. "You aren't my nurse anymore. And if I do have a wife out there, I think I would remember. And if I was so important to her, how come she hasn't tried to find me? Maybe I don't know who I was before, but I know who I am right now. Right now, I am with you."

I couldn't argue with him anymore, as he reached over and ran his fingers through my hair, sending shivers down my spine. Then he kissed me again. He kissed me as we walked into the house and upstairs to my room. This time, I didn't try to stop him. Any worries I might have had just disappeared that night, and I knew there was no turning back.

CHAPTER

20

The next morning, I woke up to the smell of food cooking. I rolled over and rubbed my eyes sleepily. I reached over and felt that John's side of the bed was still warm. I got up and walked out to the kitchen, where he stood over the stove, cooking some sausage in a skillet. When he saw me, he looked up and smiled.

"Good morning. Did you sleep well?"

I nodded. "Like a baby. And you?"

He flipped the sausage, and then he turned to look at me. "I slept better than I have since the accident. I think it helped that I had the most beautiful lady in the world beside me."

I smiled at the compliment. "Well, I don't know about that." I grabbed a mug and poured myself a cup of coffee. "Listen, John, we need to talk about last night."

A worried look came over his face. "I hope you're not having second thoughts, because I'm sure not."

I shook my head, "No, but I do think we should take things slow. I really like you, but I don't want to rush into anything, either. Like I said, I don't take this sort of thing lightly."

He nodded. "I understand. Just so you know, I wasn't exactly planning this; it just happened. But I'm glad it did."

We both smiled at each other, and then he put his arms around me and kissed me. I knew that there was no denying it, I was falling for him. And I could tell he felt the same way about me.

John and I had breakfast together. There was a sort of relaxed silence between us as we ate. Neither one of us needed to say anything. After breakfast, he went back to his place while I did a little housework. I dusted, vacuumed, and did the laundry. I made sure to wash Danny's green school shirt, so he could wear it Monday morning for school spirit day. I didn't want any trouble like last week. I found myself humming cheerfully as I folded a load of laundry, and I realized I hadn't been this happy in a very long time. I had tried to convince myself that I didn't need a man to make me happy, and maybe I didn't. But still, it was nice to have someone there to talk to and have fun with. After things went so sour with David, I had put walls up, vowing to never let anyone hurt me again. But there was something about John that was making them come down, and that was scary and exciting all at the same time.

After I'd finished my morning chores, I went out to the backyard to do some watering. The recent heat wave had left the lawn very dry. John came out to join me, with a pitcher of lemonade. We visited as we sipped on it, and it was relaxing with the conversation always flowing freely. After a while, we were both sweating. John looked at me with a mischievous grin, and then he went over and grabbed the hose.

"Oh no, you don't!" I laughed, putting up my hands to defend myself, but he aimed it right at me, and before I knew it, I was drenched. He laughed gleefully.

"Oh, you're gonna get it now!" I joked, and I grabbed Danny's Super Soaker water gun and aimed it at him. He started to run away, but I soaked him good. Pretty soon, we were in a full-blown water fight, laughing and soaking each other like a couple of grade-school kids. I was sopping wet, but I couldn't remember the last time I had had that much fun.

Later that evening, I started browning hamburger for spaghetti, while I waited for Danny to come home. The house was cleaner than it had been for a while, and all of the laundry was done. I had even had time to do a couple of loads of John's laundry after our water fight. It had been a good weekend, but I still couldn't wait for Danny to get home. I always felt as if a little part of me was missing when he was away.

At six o clock on the dot, he came bouncing up to the door, with David walking behind him. I thought that was odd, because David rarely came to the door when he dropped Danny off.

"Hi, Mom!" Danny called as he ran into the kitchen. "Where's John?"

I laughed. "What am I, chopped liver? He's in the guest house. I think he's taking a shower, but he'll be over in a little while."

He nodded, with a look of disappointment on his face. Then David walked up behind him, and he gave me a cold stare.

"Hey, Danny, why don't you go to your room for a minute? I want to talk to your mom about something."

Danny gave me a quick hug before he ran off to his room, and I looked at David, puzzled. "What's up?"

"I think you know what's up," he said coolly. "Danny says some guy is staying in the guest house."

I nodded. "Uh-huh. I'm surprised you didn't see it on the news. He's a patient of mine who needed a place to stay, so—"

"Well, I don't think it's very responsible of you to take somebody in who you hardly know," he cut me off, his words sounded angry. "I'm not so sure I like the idea of some guy hanging out with Danny. And he told me this guy even stayed with him while you were at work—is that true?"

"Yes," I said. Something about his words enraged me. "Danny was suspended, and I had to work. They had a really great time together. John actually enjoys spending time with him, which is more than I can say for you! They built a tree house together; Danny has wanted one of those for as long as I can remember. And I don't see why this is any of your business, anyway! You lost the right to have any control over my personal life when you cheated on me with Carolyn. Or did you forget that teeny little fact?"

He sighed and shook his head. "No, I haven't forgotten. How could I? You remind me all the time. I have told you I'm sorry more times than I can count. I thought we were past that."

I noticed that the hamburger meat was smoking, and I ran over to stir it. "No, David, we will never be past that. Saying you're sorry doesn't fix all the damage you have done. Now, is there anything else you want to lecture me about, because I would really like to get on with my evening."

He cleared his throat before he continued. "Actually, there was something important I wanted to talk to you about. My company is opening a new branch in New York, and I was offered a job there. I will be making a lot more money if I decide to take it."

"Well, don't let me stop you," I said. "Go ahead and take it."

He nodded. "I probably will, but here's the thing. I think Danny should come with us. I really don't think you're making good choices recently when it comes to him. Besides, Carolyn and I can offer him something you can't—a stable two-parent family and siblings. I've already contacted a lawyer."

I felt my face turning red, and I took a deep breath before I spoke. "Take Danny with you? You don't even know him! I'm the one who stayed up all night with him when he was sick! I'm the one who has put him first since the day he was born. You're just doing this as some sort of power trip, and it's not going to work! You can go to New York if you want, but Danny stays with me. Period!" I walked over to the door, opened it, and gestured for him to leave.

"I thought you might say that," he said as he walked to the door. "But I'm not giving up without a fight, and I think I have a pretty good chance. My lawyer will be contacting you." With that, he walked out the door, and I slammed it behind him. I turned around, banged my fist on the counter, and screamed. Just then I looked up to see John and Danny standing in the doorway, with concerned looks on both their faces.

"Mom, are you okay?" Danny asked.

I took some deep breaths to calm myself down. "Yes, I'm fine, son. Just a little misunderstanding with your father." I went to add the pasta to the boiling water, and John came up behind me and put his hand on my shoulder.

"Are you sure you're okay?"

I nodded. "I will be. We can talk about it later, okay?" I didn't want to go into detail about my conversation with David in front of Danny; I knew that would only upset him.

"Well, I'm starved," said Danny. "When is dinner?"

A little while later the three of us sat down to eat. I'd made French bread and salad to go with the spaghetti. We were quiet for a while, enjoying the food. Every once in a while, John would look at me and smile, and I would smile back. Danny looked at us with a puzzled expression.

"You two keep looking at each other funny. Is there something going on?"

I laughed. "Why would you say that?"

He shrugged. "I don't know. You just seem different, I guess. So what did you do this weekend?"

John and I looked at each other, an expression of guilt on both our faces. "Oh, nothing."

Later that night, after Danny was in bed, John and I sat on the couch together and watched reruns of some old comedy shows. I was still thinking about my talk with David, and John could tell something was the matter. He looked at me, clearly concerned.

"So, Jen, you never told me what was wrong, earlier. Did Danny's father say something to upset you?"

I grabbed the remote and turned off the TV. "I didn't want to say anything in front of Danny, but his father plans to take a job in New York, and he wants to take Danny with him."

A look of rage came over his face. "What! Take him to New York? From what I've heard, that guy doesn't even care about Danny enough to spend quality time with him every other weekend. Why would he want to keep him permanently? Unless he has a problem with me being here. That's it, isn't it? He doesn't want Danny spending time with me."

I shook my head. "I don't want you to blame yourself. David will always try to find a way to get under my skin; it's just who he is. It's his way of controlling the situation, but it's not going to work. There's no way he is taking Danny anywhere. I'll make sure of that."

He smiled. "You are one tough lady, you know that?"

"Yep," I said playfully. "So don't mess with me, or else." Then he kissed me, and all of my worries just disappeared.

CHAPTER 21

When my alarm went off on Monday morning, I moaned and hit the snooze button. After such a busy weekend, I wasn't ready for it to end and another week to begin. I'd hoped I would be able to go to work and give Melissa the good news that I'd talked to Doctor Furguson and that he would be able to do the surgery that would save her from being paralyzed, or worse. I'd promised her husband I would do everything I could to make that happen. But now I would have to tell her that there was nothing I could do. This was the part of my job I didn't like. I hated to give people bad news. After the alarm had gone off three times, I decided it was time to get up and face my day. We were having our reviews soon, so I couldn't miss work, and Danny couldn't miss school, either, especially after having already missed nearly a week when he was suspended. So I dragged myself out of my bed and jumped into the shower. The water felt so good, I probably stayed in a little too long, especially since I was already running behind. I dried off and dressed in my lavender scrubs. When I went down to the kitchen, Danny was sitting at the kitchen table, watching cartoons and eating a bowl of cereal. He looked up briefly during the commercial break.

"Good morning, Mom."

"Good morning, Danny." I went to pour a cup of coffee and a bowl of cereal for myself. Danny was wearing his green school shirt, and I could tell he'd already combed his hair. I was pleased that he was already dressed and ready for his day. Just a year ago that wouldn't have happened. I would have had to drag him out of bed. It was proof that he was maturing, and I knew I had something to do with that. I watched Danny as he ate his cereal, and I thought again about what David had said, that I wasn't making good choices for him. That made my blood boil. Who did he think he was? It was ridiculous for him to think he would be a better parent than I was. He knew nothing about Danny! He didn't even like him. I would show him! He had no idea who he was messing with. If he wanted a fight, I would give him a good one. I would make it so he'd never see Danny again.

Just then, my thoughts were interrupted by a knock at the door. Danny continued to stare at the TV screen, expressionless. I opened it, and there stood John, looking especially handsome in a nice pair of slacks and collared shirt. He smiled, and something about that smile just made me melt.

"Good morning, Jen."

"Good morning." I motioned for him to come in. He walked in and waved to Danny, who looked up with a big grin and waved back.

"Listen, my co-worker just called me, and he's sick today. Do you think you could give me a lift to work?"

I looked at the clock on the wall and sighed. I was already running behind, and I really couldn't risk being late to work. Not with reviews coming up. But what was a few more minutes? Besides, I couldn't say no to John.

"Okay, but we need to hurry. We can't be late today."

On the way to drop John off, he and Danny chatted like a couple of old pals. Danny talked about school, and John told him about his job at the grocery outlet. I was glad that they had become so close. Danny needed a good male role model, someone who actually took the time to listen to him. After I had dropped John off, I drove to the school.

Danny bounced out of the car and ran toward his classroom. I smiled as I watched Tommy walk up to him. They entered the classroom together, laughing as if they were best friends. You'd never know that, not very long ago, they had been mortal enemies.

I arrived to work that day with just seconds to spare. After I punched in my time card, I ran to the nurses' station to grab the patients' files. Lisa looked up and smiled when she saw me.

"Hey, Jen. I hear you're quite the miracle worker." I wrinkled my brow. "Why would you say that?"

She shrugged. "Well, you went and talked to Doctor Furguson this weekend, didn't you?"

I nodded. "Yes, but it really didn't do any good. As a matter of fact, I think he's kind of a jerk."

Lisa turned pale as a ghost, and she pointed behind me. I turned around to see Doctor Furguson standing there, and I almost fainted.

"Good morning, Jennifer."

"Good morning," I muttered. "I didn't mean, I—."

He put up his hand and shook his head. "Don't worry about it. You're right; I was kind of a jerk the other day, and I want to apologize for that. But ever since you came to my office, I've been thinking about your patient, Melissa. I was up all night racking my brain, thinking about a way that I could help her. And I think I can remove her tumors, without damaging her spine or brain. It would be the most challenging job I've ever done, but I think it can be done. I was just talking with Melissa about the risks and benefits of surgery, and she's all for it. From the looks of things, I'd say the sooner, the better."

I let out a sigh of relief, and then I smiled. "Thank you."

He nodded. "No problem. I was also thinking about what you said about my mom. You were right, and I'm going to try to lighten my load so I can spend more time with her. I've already canceled all of my patients for the next few weeks, so I can perform the surgery on Melissa, and I can stay with Mom while I'm here. That way, I can get a better idea of how she's doing, and how much help she really needs."

I beamed, thinking to myself that this day just couldn't get much better.

When I went to check on Melissa a little while later, she looked better than she had in a while. She must have thanked me at least ten times for talking to Doctor Furguson. She said that I had given her something no one else could—hope. It was at moments like this that I really loved my job, and I couldn't imagine doing anything else. I walked around for most of the day on cloud nine, until I ran into Doctor Martin in the hallway. He had a disappointed look on his face, and I just knew it wasn't good.

"Jen, can I talk to you for a minute?"

"Sure." I followed him into his office and sat in the chair across from him. He was silent for a few minutes, deep in thought. When he finally spoke, his voice was stern.

"So, I hear you went to San Francisco to talk to Doctor Furguson about Melissa?"

I nodded. "Yes, sir. I thought he could help her."

He nodded. "I understand, and I know your heart is in the right place." He reached into his desk and pulled out a file. It had a name written on it. Sherry Johnson. I had never heard of that person before, and I wondered where Dr. Martin was going with this. He cleared his throat. "This is a patient I treated years ago, before you worked here. I was a lot like you back then. I wanted to be the miracle worker. She had many inoperable tumors, just as Melissa does. I took it upon myself to find a surgeon who was willing to operate. She died during that operation, but if I had left things alone, she might have lived longer. He looked down and shook his head sadly. She had a husband and two kids. Needless to say, her husband wasn't happy that she died, when she could have been with him a little longer. He sued the hospital for negligence, and I could have lost everything I worked so hard for." He reached into the file and pulled out a family picture of a young-looking couple and two children. We both stared at the picture for a while in silence, and then he continued. "I know you all think I am some kind of monster, but I care about these patients just as much as you do. I just want you to realize that it can go the other way, too."

I had never seen this side of Doctor Martin before. I had always thought of him as a heartless jerk, but now he seemed almost human. As I watched the tears puddle up in his eyes, I put my hand on his shoulder.

"That patient might not have made it, but sometimes you have to take risks. I really believe in Melissa, and I think she and the baby will make it."

He looked up at me and smiled, as he put the file back into his desk. "I hope she makes it; I really do."

"She will. They both will." I stood up and was getting ready to leave, when Doctor Martin cleared his throat.

"And, Jen, just one more thing before you leave."

"What's that, sir?"

"I assume Melissa's x-rays will be back in her file by the end of the day." I smiled. "They already are."

CHAPTER

22

When I got home that evening, I started to clean and organize everything in my house. It really wasn't that dirty to begin with, but my parents were coming in the next day, and my mom was a bit of a neat freak. Everything had to be just so, or I would hear about it. Because of this, I always felt a little on edge when they came down to visit. I loved them dearly, don't get me wrong. But sometimes I was glad they only came down a couple of times a year. I could just hear my mother saying, "Your home says a lot about who you are." Danny helped me as I cleaned the kitchen and organized all of the contents.

"Do these bowls go here?" he asked.

I nodded. "Yes, and make sure to wipe out the cupboard before you put them in."

We continued to clean and organize, and then we heard a knock at the back door. I knew who it was before I opened it. John stood there, with a big smile on his face.

"Hi, how's it going?" He looked around the kitchen. "Are you two doing a little spring cleaning?"

"Sort of," I answered. "My parents are coming down from Florida tomorrow. My mom's a little bit of a neat freak, so I'm just trying to tidy up a bit."

He nodded. "I'm looking forward to meeting them. Is there anything I can do to help?"

I looked around the kitchen.

"Well, some of those dishes go on the top shelf, and I have a hard time reaching it, if you don't mind."

"I don't mind at all."

After we were done cleaning and organizing, we decided to go to our favorite Chinese restaurant for dinner. Danny and I had gone there for years, and they knew us by name. When we arrived, the owner, June, greeted us with a warm smile.

"Hi, it's good to see you again. Dinner for three tonight?" She looked at John with curiosity.

"Yes," I said. "This is my friend John."

She nodded and shook John's hand. "Good to meet you. Follow me this way." June led us to a large table near the window. "The best seat in the house for my favorite customers." We all sat down, and she handed us our menus. "Can I get you started with something to drink?"

"I'll have a root beer!" Danny called cheerfully. June scribbled that down and then looked at John and me.

I thought it over for a minute. "I think I'll have that beer you brought out last time we were here."

John smiled. "That sounds good. I'll have the same."

"No problem. I'll give you a few minutes to look over the menu, okay?" She went off to help another customer.

John picked up his menu and started looking it over. "This seems like a great place."

"It really is. Danny and I have come here since he was a baby. They have watched him grow up."

Danny nodded. "And they even gave me one of those cool Chinese lanterns to hang in my room." He pointed toward a red lantern hanging in the far corner. "Sometimes, they even bring out free samples for us to try."

As if on cue, our waitress came walking out with our drinks, and a sample of salt and pepper green beans.

John looked impressed. "I like this place more already."

We all enjoyed our meal, laughing and talking as we ate. I liked John more and more all the time, and I felt lucky to have him in my life. It was probably crazy for me to feel that way, since he didn't even remember who he was. But I had feelings for him that were hard to ignore. Not only was he handsome, but he was kind and funny. Maybe it was a little odd that we had started our relationship backward. Instead of dating like a normal couple, he was living in my guest house and having dinner with us every night. I'd been on very few dates since David and I had split up, and I had never introduced anyone to Danny. I'd promised myself that I wouldn't let Danny get attached to some man, just to have him ripped from his life if it didn't work out. But John and Danny had an instant connection, and I couldn't picture it any other way. I hoped my parents liked him as much as I did.

After we'd finished dinner and paid the bill, we all broke open our fortune cookies.

Danny looked at his fortune, with a serious expression on his face. "'You will go on many incredible journeys.'" He looked up at me with a smile. "Does that mean we can go on a trip this summer?"

"Maybe, if I can get the time off from work." I looked at my own fortune. "'You will find the meaning of true love.'" John and I looked at each other, smiling.

Danny rolled his eyes. "There's that look again."

"What look?" I took a bite of my fortune cookie.

"The one you and John keep giving each other." He batted his eyes, mimicking the look, and John and I burst into laughter.

When I finally stopped laughing, I looked at John. "So what does your fortune say?"

He held it up to read it. "'You must choose your path wisely.'" He shrugged. "I have no idea what that means."

We collected our things, preparing to leave—and that was when she walked in. She was a pretty, tall brunette, with a slender build. She was wearing a very short denim skirt and a low-cut tank top. I had never seen her in my life, but she immediately locked eyes with John. The way she looked at him made it obvious that she knew him. My heart started to pound, as she walked toward us. All of my insecure feelings started to surface. Was she his girlfriend? His wife? Or a relative? Whoever she was, she sure wasn't pleased to see him. I could tell by the way she wrinkled her brow when she looked at him.

"Derek?"

John looked at her—he clearly had no idea who she was. "I'm sorry, do I know you?"

With that, her eyes filled with rage, and she slapped him right across the face. Everyone in the restaurant stared in silence. John held his hand where she had slapped him, a look of disbelief on his face. "I don't know who you are, or what I did to make you so mad, but whatever it is, I'm sorry."

"You're *sorry*? You think that makes it okay for you to promise to call me, and then leave me waiting by the phone night after night?"

He shrugged. "I was in a car accident less than a month ago, and I can't remember anything from before that time. I don't know why I would do something like that, but I'm sure there's a logical explanation."

Her expression softened a bit. "You really can't remember anything?" He shook his head sadly. "Nope. Anything that you might be able to tell me about who I was before would be very helpful."

She bit down on her bottom lip, thinking this over. "Well, I really didn't know you that well. I don't know if I could really be much help."

John had a desperate look on his face. "Anything would be more than I know right now," he pleaded.

She nodded, finally cracking a slight smile. "Okay. And my name's Sarah, by the way."

I think I held my breath the whole time John was talking to Sarah. They sat on a little bench outside the restaurant, deep in conversation. Danny and I walked around the little strip mall across the way, but I kept looking back over to them, trying to read their expressions. An uncontrollable feeling of jealousy came over me, and it confirmed how strong my feelings for him really were. What if he decided his feelings for this woman, Sarah, were stronger than his feelings for me? I tried my best to shake those thoughts away as I peeked through the window of a woman's clothing store, admiring a pretty white dress.

Danny looked up at me, concerned. "Who was that lady, Mom? And how come she was so mad at John?"

"I don't know, son. That's what John is trying to figure out." We continued to walk around, looking into the windows of the little shops. We came to a little toy store, and Danny's eyes lit up when he saw a remote-control helicopter. He had wanted one for a long time, but they were expensive.

"I sure would love one of those for my birthday." I could tell from the tone in his voice that he knew he wasn't going to get one. Between the mortgage and all of my other bills, we were barely scraping by. Although I tried not to discuss finances in front of Danny, he was a smart kid. He saw the hopeless look on my face when I paid the bills. And he saw that while some kids in his class had all the newest toys and video game systems, we didn't have any of that. He never complained, though. That was one of his attributes that made me feel lucky to be his mother.

"We'll see," I told him as I put my arm around him.

Just then, John and Sarah stood up. They shook hands and smiled at each other, and she got in her car and drove away. My heart started pounding again as John walked back toward us. I wondered what they had said, how well she knew him, and if John had found out anything about his life before the accident. He smiled as he came closer, and he walked up and put his arm around me.

"Let's go home."

A little while later, after Danny was in bed, John and I were sitting on the couch together. We were quiet for a while, until I finally blurted it out.

"So, what did Sarah say?" That question had been on my mind since we'd left the restaurant, but I hadn't wanted to discuss it in front of Danny.

He took a deep breath before he spoke. "Well, she's a girl I dated briefly a few years ago. I guess we met at a bar and went out a few times. She says my name was Derek, but she didn't know my last name. She doesn't know where I lived, either, since I always picked her up at her house. I guess she really had feelings for me, but I just stopped calling her. I apologized, of course. It doesn't seem like something I would do."

I nodded. "So, did you remember anything when you saw her?" He shook his head. "Nope. I was really hoping I would."

I was silent for a moment before I spoke again. "Do you think you will see her again?"

John looked me in the eye, a slight smile on his face. He knew exactly what I was thinking. "There is no reason to see her again. There is only one woman in my life right now, and she's sitting right here in front of me." He leaned in and kissed me, and I relaxed a little. I kissed him back, but there were still questions on my mind that I couldn't ignore. I pulled away, giving him my most serious look.

"There are still some things we need to talk about."

He leaned back in the couch and crossed his arms over his chest. "Like what?"

"Like this thing between us." I gestured at the space between us.

He looked at me with a curious expression. "What about it? Because I think it's pretty great."

I nodded. "I know, and I'm not denying that. But you and I both know it's complicated."

He raised his hands defensively. "It's only as complicated as you want to make it. I like you, and you like me. We enjoy spending time together. Is that really so complicated?"

I shook my head, "No, but there's more to it than that."

"Like what?"

"Like the fact that you don't know who you were three weeks ago. And if you would walk out on Sarah, how do you know you wouldn't do that to me? And it's not just me who's involved now. I have to think about Danny."

He took a deep breath before he spoke. "You have every right to worry about that, and I can't say I would blame you if you told me to find another place to stay. I might not know who I was three weeks ago, but I know who I am right now. And that's because of you. Your kindness has taught me more than you will ever know. You are an amazing mother, and an incredible nurse, and to top it all off, you're drop-dead gorgeous." He smiled, and I felt me cheeks get hot. He reached over and ran his fingers through my hair before he continued. "I know in my heart that I would never do anything to hurt you or Danny. And I would love it if we could spend more time together and see where this thing between us might take us."

I felt my knees turn into jelly as we kissed. It was the most passionate kiss I'd ever had, and I knew at that moment that I had completely, totally fallen for him. I couldn't make my feelings for him go away, even if I wanted to. But I still had one more question left.

"So, do I call you John or Derek?"

He laughed. "Call me John. I like that name."

We both smiled, and he kissed me again. We made love that night before we fell asleep in each other's arms.

CHAPTER 23

I danced into work the next day, feeling light as a feather. It was going to be a great day; I could feel it. I was only working until noon, so I could pick up my parents from the airport, and I had scheduled the next few days off as well. I couldn't wait for my parents to meet John. I knew that it would take our relationship to a whole new level. I wondered again if he had any family out there, and if he did, why none of them had come forward. After all, the story had been all over the news. But I tried to push those thoughts out of my head and focus on the positive. We had a fun-filled week ahead of us. We planned to go to the county fair and the jazz festival in Old Sacramento. My parents always loved going to the jazz festival when they were in town, and Danny was excited about the fair, so it was a win-win situation.

I had spent most of the morning preparing the guest room for my parent's arrival. John had offered to move his things out of the guest house so my parents could stay there, but I wasn't sure how they would react to him staying in the house with me. My mom was already a little leery about him, and my dad was just a little overprotective. He had never approved of anyone I'd dated. "No one is good enough for my little girl," he would say. After he found out David had been cheating on me, he had been livid. He'd followed him home one night and punched him right in the face. David had threatened to file charges, but he never did. He'd always been a little intimidated by my dad, and I think that, deep down, he knew he deserved it.

I focused my mind back on my job and went to Melissa's room, where I discovered that she was in surgery. I was happy and nervous, all at the same time. I remembered what Doctor Martin had told me, and I hoped everything would go well for Melissa and her unborn baby. I was the one who had gone to find doctor Furguson, and even though he was the one performing the surgery, I felt responsible. As I went back to the nurses' station, I saw Mrs. Furguson sitting there waiting for me. She looked better than she had for a while. There was a glow about her and a light in her eyes that I had never seen before.

"Hi, Mrs. Furguson," I said. "How are you today?"

"I'm doing great," she answered. "I just wanted to come by and thank you for talking to my son. We have had the best time together since he came to town, and I know he came because of what you said to him. He's even thinking about starting a practice right here in Sacramento."

I beamed. "That is great news."

The morning flew by. I checked on all of my patients, just as I always did: a man with stomach pain, a woman recovering from an auto accident, and a young man who was recovering from a gunshot wound to the shoulder. It was a gang-related shooting, and I had seen the story on the news that morning. He was only eighteen and at the head of his class, with his whole life ahead of him. I wondered how he had ended up going down the wrong path. He didn't say much when I went to his room to check on him, and he hadn't had any visitors since he'd been admitted. I thought to myself that the lack of family support was probably exactly the reason he had started hanging out with the wrong people. It made me glad that Danny had bonded with John. Even though I tried to be the best mother possible to him, every boy needed a strong male role model, and I knew he wasn't getting that from his father.

At twelve o clock, I went to the staff room to collect my things. I was just headed out the door, when I saw Doctor Furguson walking down the hall. I knew he had probably just finished up with Melissa's surgery, and I was curious to know how it had gone. I tried to read his expression, but the only thing I noticed was how tired he looked. He let out a big sigh and wiped the sweat from his brow.

"Hi," I said. "How did Melissa's surgery go?"

He cracked a slight smile. "Well, as good as can be expected. It was a little trickier than I thought. One of the tumors was completely wrapped around her spine. I think I got it all, but there's a lot of swelling. We'll just have to wait until after the swelling goes down to see if she can move her legs. Melissa's a fighter, though. I have confidence that she will pull through this. She's in recovery now, and she seems to be resting comfortably. Her husband is with her."

I nodded. "Thanks again for doing this. I know it wasn't easy for you to come here."

He put his hand on my shoulder. "I'm the one who should be thanking you."

CHAPTER 24

When I arrived at the airport to pick up my parents, it was alive with activity. People were greeting friends and family members, hugging, and crying happy tears. It was heartwarming to see. I had picked up Danny early from school, so he could come with me, and of course, he was as happy to have an early day as I was. He stood beside me, watching the people exit from their flights.

"They should be coming out any minute now," I told him. He nodded and continued to watch intently as people passed by. Some were entire families, others were people traveling alone. As I watched a family of four walking hand in hand, I thought about how nice it would be for Danny and me to have that. I had always dreamed that I would marry my Prince Charming and live happily ever after, with a white picket fence and a couple of kids. It's amazing how dreams can change in the blink of an eye.

It seemed like we had been standing there forever before I finally saw my parents walking toward us. My mother was wearing a cute green shorts outfit, and my dad was wearing the Sacramento Kings jersey I had given him for his birthday last year. He had always been a Kings fan, even after he moved to Florida. They both had big smiles on their faces, and Danny ran to them and hugged them both.

My mother inspected him from head to toe. "This can't be Danny—he's way too big."

Danny laughed. "It's me, Grandma."

"Well, of course it is. But you must have grown at least a foot since the last time I saw you."

Danny beamed with pride, and I went closer and gave each of my parents a hug and kiss. "Good to see you."

"We're happy to be here," said my dad. "Well, everything we brought was carry-on, so let's get going."

A short while later we arrived home. I showed my parents to the guest room and helped them get settled in. I had worked hard the day before cleaning the guest room, and I felt proud as I looked around. The carpet was accented with fresh vacuum lines, and there wasn't a speck of dust.

"The house looks great, sweetheart," said my dad.

"Thanks. Danny and I cleaned it yesterday."

He looked out the window toward the guest house. "So, when are we going to meet this mystery man of yours?"

I smiled. "Soon, I promise. I'm going to make a pot roast for dinner tonight, and he will be joining us. And Daddy?"

"What?"

"Just don't give him the third degree. I really like this guy, and I don't want you to scare him away. That goes for you too, Mom."

She put her hand to her chest with a shocked expression on her face. "Who, me? I would never do that."

I rolled my eyes. "You always do that. I just want a nice, peaceful dinner, okay?"

They both nodded. "Okay."

I was chopping the carrots a little while later, when John knocked on the back door. My parents were in the living room, watching something on the game show network and playing a game of Uno with Danny.

I was excited and nervous about them meeting John. He'd become a very important person in my life, and I wanted everything to go well.

When I opened the door, John was standing there holding a dozen red roses. "These are for you."

I suddenly felt as if I were back in high school. I gently took the roses and smelled them, taking in the sweet scent. "Thank you. Let me get a vase for these." I went over to the cabinet and pulled out a pretty crystal vase I had gotten for Christmas from a patient a few years back. I had started to arrange the roses in the vase, when John put his arms around me and kissed me. I was amazed at how I felt weak in the knees every time he kissed me.

"I can't wait to meet your parents," he said with a smile.

"Well, they're looking forward to meeting you, too." I led John out to the living room. Danny and my parents were still engrossed in their game of Uno.

"Uno!" Danny cheered. They all looked up at us, and it was quiet for a moment before I spoke.

"John, this is my mother, Catherine, and my father, Roger. Mom and Dad, this is John."

"Nice to meet you," said my mother.

My father got up to shake his hand. "Danny's been telling us a lot of good things about you. He says you helped him build that tree house out back."

John smiled. "It was easy, wasn't it, Danny?" Danny nodded in agreement. "Piece of cake."

My dad ruffled Danny's hair and gave John a look of approval. "Well, any friend of Danny's is a friend of ours. It really is good to meet you, John."

John let out a sigh of relief. "Good to meet you, too."

Later that evening, as we all sat around the dinner table, everyone seemed to be enjoying their food in a comfortable silence.

"This is delicious," my mom complimented.

I scooped another serving of potatoes onto my plate. "Thanks, Mom." Then she turned to John, with a curious expression on her face. "So, I hear you work at the grocery store."

John nodded as he finished chewing his food. "Yes, and it's worked out really well. I get a discount on all of my groceries that way, and I've met some really nice people, too."

"That's good." She cut her meat up into tiny pieces, deep in thought for a minute before she spoke again. "I just have one question."

John looked up at her. "What?"

"How come you seem so calm? I mean, if I'd forgotten everything, I think I would be a nervous wreck."

My dad narrowed his eyes at her. "Catherine, I don't think that's an appropriate question."

John shook his head. "That's a good question, actually. I think I would be a mess if it weren't for these two." He gestured toward Danny and me. "I don't know what I would have done if Jen hadn't taken me in the way she did. She gave me the chance to start from scratch." He looked at me and smiled. "You should be proud of your daughter; she really is quite a woman."

My dad beamed. "We know that. Jen has been special from the day she was born. I could just tell, even then, that she was going to do great things.

She has a heart of gold, and she's smart, too. It's hard to find that all in one package."

I felt my cheeks turning red. "Aw, Daddy. I think you're supposed to say those things."

He speared another piece of meat on his fork. "I'm only telling the truth, sweetheart. And anyone with half a brain would agree with me."

John looked up from his plate. "I agree with you 100 percent." He raised his glass and held it toward the center of the table. "I'd like to make a toast to Jen, just for being the incredible woman that she is."

Everyone else raised their glasses and clinked them together. "To Jen."

CHAPTER

25

The next day was another scorcher. Even with the air conditioner running full blast, I still woke up drenched in my own sweat. We had planned to go to the county fair, and I knew Danny would be anxious to get there, so I took a quick shower and put on my coolest sundress. It was peach with white flowers on it, and I liked the way it looked on me. I put on some makeup and headed down to the kitchen, where Danny was eating a donut and watching cartoons.

"That's a healthy breakfast," I joked.

He shrugged. "Grandma said I could have one."

"Of course she did." My mom always loved to let Danny do whatever he wanted when she was around, and he knew it. But he only saw them a couple times a year, and a few extra cookies and donuts never hurt anyone.

Danny finished chewing his donut and took a drink of his milk. "Is it almost time to go to the fair?"

"Almost." I poured myself a cup of coffee and grabbed a donut out of the box on the counter. *If you can't beat them, join them*, I thought to myself.

* * *

When we arrived at the fair, it was busy, just as it always was on opening weekend. Danny bounced through the gates as if he were floating on air. He always looked forward to the fair, and we'd gone every year since he was a baby. He wasn't a big fan of the rides, as most kids his age were, but he loved the exhibits. All around us were the typical sights and sounds of the fair. Carnival workers called out to everyone who passed by, trying to get them to play a game, promising that 'You will get a prize even if you lose.' That's the biggest load of bull I ever heard. (Maybe after you have given them fifty dollars you might get the tiniest little prize they have.) There was the sound of excited people screaming on the big roller coaster, and the smell of delicious deep-fried carnival food filled the air. This definitely wasn't the place to be if you were trying to diet.

"I want to see the animals first!" said Danny as he skipped ahead of us.

"Okay," I said, following his lead.

We headed for the big building that housed the pigs, goats, and sheep. None of the animals looked as if they wanted to be there; most were sleeping in a corner of their pens. We circled the building, looking at all of the animals, although after a while they all started to look alike. My parents and John seemed to be getting along. They were chatting as we walked around. I knelt down to pet a cute little baby goat when someone came up behind me.

"Hi, guys!" I turned around to see Tommy's mom, Stacy, standing there.

Tommy was already standing with Danny, looking at some pigs.

"Hi," I said. "Good to see you."

She nodded. "Good to see you, too. Tommy and I come here every year."

"Danny and I do, too." I looked at the boys, who were laughing and talking like best friends. "I'm glad to see they are getting along now."

"Me, too," she agreed. "I'm still really sorry for what Tommy did to Danny."

"Don't worry about it."

"Well, thank you for being so understanding. Tommy is doing so much better now, and I think Danny has something to do with that. He's been a really good friend to him. You're doing a great job with him; you should be proud."

"I am. Listen, since we're all here together, you two can hang out with us if you like. I think the boys would like that."

She beamed. "I would love to."

I introduced Tommy and his mom to John and my parents, and we all had a great time together that afternoon. We walked through all of the exhibits, had fried food for lunch, and Danny even went on a few rides with Tommy. I was glad to see Danny having so much fun with someone his own age. He'd spent so much time with adults, I worried sometimes that he didn't know how to interact with other kids. But seeing him and Tommy together that day, I felt all of those concerns just vanish. I liked his mom a lot, too. She was someone I could see myself being friends with for a very long time. I thought again about how she had lost her husband, and I wondered how I would react if I were in the same situation. I looked at John and smiled. I felt lucky to have him in my life. He took my hand as we walked through the fairgrounds, and I felt more relaxed than I had in years.

* * * *

I had a hard time sleeping that night. I tried every trick in the book, and I still couldn't fall asleep. After what seemed like hours of tossing and turning, I wandered out to the kitchen to get a drink of water. My dad was sitting at the table, having some cookies and milk.

"What are you doing awake?" he asked.

"I couldn't sleep."

He shrugged. "Me neither. Do you want some?" He gestured toward the half-empty bag of chocolate-chip cookies.

I smiled. "I would love some."

I sat down beside my dad, and he poured me a glass of milk. It made me feel as if I were five years old again. When I was still living at home, my father and I would sometimes have a snack together in the middle of the night. My mom, who could sleep through a hurricane, had been oblivious to it all. We both munched on our cookies quietly for a while, enjoying the moment. Then I thought of something I'd been meaning to ask him.

"Hey, Dad, do you still have the number for that lawyer friend of yours?" He nodded. "I think so. Why?"

I finished chewing my cookie and wiped my face with a napkin. "Well, I didn't want to say anything in front of Danny, but his father is going to be moving to New York soon, and he wants to take Danny with him."

"What?" He almost choked on the cookie he was eating. "There's no way he's taking my grandson anywhere!"

I put my finger to my lips to quiet him. I didn't want to wake anyone up. "That's exactly what I told him. I think he's just mad about John staying here, and so he's going on some sort of power trip. I don't know if he's really going to go through with it, but I want to be prepared, just in case."

He nodded. "Well, I'm pretty sure I still have my friend's business card in my wallet. I'll make sure to give it to you before we leave."

"Thanks, Dad."

He smiled. "No problem. Now I think it's time for us to try and get some sleep, don't you?"

I nodded, and we both carried our glasses to the sink.

"Goodnight, Dad."

"Goodnight, Jen."

CHAPTER

26

I had such a great visit with my parents, I was a little sad when it was time for them to leave on Sunday afternoon. Although they had both been skeptical about John at first, they were raving about him when I dropped them off at the airport.

My dad grabbed his bag out of the trunk and flung it over his shoulder. "Thanks for having us. We had a really good time, sweetheart."

I gave them both a hug. "Maybe next time, Danny and I can fly out to see you."

Danny's eyes lit up. "Really, Mom?"

I nodded. "Sure, it's been a while since we've flown out there. It would be fun."

"Can John come, too?" He looked at my parents for approval.

My mom smiled. "Sure, why not? The more the merrier. I really like John. He seems to make you and your mom really happy. And he must be strong, too. I can't imagine starting from scratch like that."

My father nodded in agreement. "He's a very nice man. I approve, and that's saying a lot, coming from me. You know I'm just a little overprotective when it comes to you."

I smiled. "I will tell him you said that."

My father hugged me one more time. I noticed there were tears in his eyes, but he quickly wiped them away before anyone noticed. "Well, we have a plane to catch."

"Okay," I said. "Call me as soon as you land."

"We will." I watched as they walked to the passenger gates, and I put my arm around Danny as we walked toward the car. "Let's go home."

* * * *

Later, at home, Danny was playing in his tree house while John cooked some shrimp skewers on the barbecue. The aroma filled the air, and it made me realize how hungry I really was. It wasn't as hot as it had been; there was a nice cool delta breeze in the air.

John took a drink of his beer and looked up at me with a smile. "One of my co—workers gave me this recipe; I hope you like it."

"I know I will," I said. "I love shrimp, and so does Danny."

"Good." He grabbed his tongs from the side of the barbecue and flipped the shrimp. "I had a really nice visit with your parents. I like them a lot."

I nodded. "They like you, too. And my dad usually can't stand anyone I date, so you should take that as a compliment."

"I do." He was quiet for a moment, staring at the shrimp. "I hope you know how much this all means to me. If it weren't for you, I wouldn't have a place to belong. You and Danny have made me a part of the family, and you didn't have to do that. I think most people would have just turned the other way."

I took a sip of the wine I'd been drinking. "Well, I'm not like most people. But I'm not perfect, either. I do have my flaws."

He raised an eyebrow. "Oh, really? If you do, then I sure haven't seen them."

I laughed. "You just haven't known me very long. I just happen to have a nasty temper. Most of the time, I'm as nice as nice can be, but if you make me mad, you'd better watch out."

He smiled. "So what happens? Does your head spin around, while green stuff flies out of your mouth?"

"It's not quite that dramatic, but it's not pretty," I said. "Only two people have made me that mad. One was my ex-husband, and the other was Doctor Martin. But it turns out I had him all wrong."

"Who, your ex-husband?" John started to pull the shrimp skewers off the barbecue and put them on a plate.

I laughed. "No, I was right about him. But I think Doctor Martin is just misunderstood. I had a talk with him, and I think I see him in a whole new light."

John nodded. "Have you heard anything about your patient, Melissa?"

I shook my head. "Nope. No news is good news, I guess. I will see how she's doing at work tomorrow." I sighed. After such a long weekend, I wasn't ready to go back to work. Just then, I noticed a loose shrimp that had fallen onto the plate, and I picked it up and popped it into my mouth. "This is so good. You should really be a professional chef."

He beamed. "I'm glad you like it. Well, everything's ready, so let's eat."

As we sat down for dinner, an overwhelming sense of peace came over me. It felt as if the three of us were a family. John was everything I had been hoping for, and I just knew he was meant to be with us. Maybe he couldn't remember who he had been before, and who knew when those memories might come flooding back. But for now, he was all mine. Sometimes in life you have to learn to live in the moment. If you let go of all your worries about the past and future, great things can happen. I think that's one of the main things he taught me. Even if he were to disappear tomorrow, he'd already given me so much.

CHAPTER 27

Monday morning, I was back to work. Although part of me didn't want to go back after such a long break, I was looking forward to checking on Melissa. I'd been thinking about her, and it would be good so see how she was doing. I was sipping my coffee and going through papers at the nurses' station, when I heard a voice.

"Hi, Jen." I looked up and saw Melissa walking toward me. I let out a big sigh of relief.

"Well, look at you."

She grinned from ear to ear. "I was a little scared, at first. When I woke up after the surgery, I couldn't feel my legs. But yesterday I started to move them, and today I'm walking. The doctors are all shocked. They didn't expect such a quick recovery."

I smiled. "It doesn't surprise me at all."

She looked deep in thought for a moment. "I want to thank you again, for talking to Doctor Furguson. If it weren't for you, I don't think he would have done the surgery. And I think Mrs. Furguson is thrilled to have her son around again."

I looked around. "Is he still here?"

She shook her head. "I think he took his mom to the jazz festival. He's supposed to check on me later today, and if everything looks good, I can go home tomorrow."

I beamed. "That's the best news I've heard in a long time."

The morning went by pretty quickly. I was surprised when I looked at the clock and saw that it was time for my lunch break. I was going to get my purse from the staff room, when I heard someone come up behind me.

"Hello, beautiful."

I spun around to see John standing there. "What are you doing here?" I asked.

"Well, I had my checkup with Doctor Martin. He gave me a clean bill of health. Of course, he can't see any reason why my memory hasn't come back yet. They did a scan of my head, and everything looks normal." He shrugged. "Anyway, I was wondering if you'd had lunch yet."

I shook my head. "I was just getting ready to take my break." He grinned from ear to ear. "Well, follow me."

John led me outside to the little area that was supposed to be used by staff during their breaks. Of course, it sat vacant, just as it did every day. It was sad that nobody really used it. Most of the employees were running around doing errands during their breaks or grabbing fast food as they rushed around. It was a nice grassy lawn shaded by a huge oak tree. I looked down to see that John had a little picnic lunch set up for us. There were sandwiches, potato chips, and even chocolate-covered strawberries for dessert. A bottle of sparkling cider and two crystal glasses topped it all off.

"Wow," I said. "How did you—"

"Don't ask how," he cut me off. "Just enjoy."

The two of us walked over and sat down on the picnic blanket. A nice breeze blew past us, and it smelled sweet, like nectar. I relaxed and started eating. I hadn't realized how hungry I was, and the food tasted so good.

"I got these from the deli at work," John said proudly. "They really do make a great sandwich."

"I agree. This was really nice of you."

He shrugged. "It's the least I could do, after everything you've done for me. Besides, it gives me more time with you."

I nodded in agreement. John and I rarely had the opportunity to be alone like this; Danny was usually with us. Not that I minded at all, it was all part of the package. When you become a parent, you give up a lot, but you gain so much more. "Well, this is sure a nice change from cafeteria food."

"I bet," he said. "If it's anything like the hospital food, the roach coach down the street would be a welcome change."

I laughed. "You're probably right."

He paused for a moment, chewing his food. "You know, I've been thinking. I want to go back to the crash site, where they found me. I think it might help me remember something."

I paused. There was a small part of me that didn't want John to remember his past. It was selfish and unreasonable, and I knew it. As long as John remained in the dark, I didn't have anyone else to compete with.

But I knew that wasn't what was best for John. He had to remember sometime.

"Okay," I said. "I can take you there after work, if you want." I had seen the coverage on the news, and I knew exactly where John's car had been found in a tangled mess.

"I appreciate that." He took my hand, and I relaxed. I was brought back into the moment with him, and my worries disappeared. We sat there, looking into each other's eyes for a minute or so, before he continued, "I want you to know that, whatever happens in the future, whoever I turn out to be, this thing between us is real. Nothing will change that, I promise."

I pulled my hand away and sighed. "Don't make promises you can't keep."

"I'm not." He kissed me, and I melted in his arms.

CHAPTER 28

After work that day, I drove John to the spot where they had found his car, in a ditch near Garden highway. I passed that spot all the time when I went to the shopping center down the road, so it wasn't hard to find. Danny had stayed after school to watch a basketball tournament with Tommy, so I had some time before I had to pick him up.

"Here we are," I said as I came to a stop.

There wasn't much to see, mostly just grass and trees. I could hear birds chattering, and there was a light breeze that blew through my hair. We both got out of the car and looked around.

John wrinkled his forehead, as if he were concentrating on something.

Then he held his hand to his head, as if it hurt.

"Are you okay?" I asked.

"I remember something!" he said. "I remember being here. And I remember hitting my head on the steering wheel when I crashed, right over there." He pointed to a shrub that had obviously been knocked down. "I can remember the white car I was driving, and how it smelled. Like a brand-new car."

He walked over to the spot, and I followed him. He was looking for something, and I pretended to help him, even though I had no idea what I was supposed to be looking for.

"So, do you remember anything else?" I questioned.

He shook his head. "No. I wish I did, but at least it's a start." He sighed. "Well, I don't think there's anything here that's going to help me; we should probably go."

We were getting ready to leave when we both noticed something at the same time. It looked like a crumpled-up piece of paper in the bushes. John reached down to pick it up, and I watched as he unwrinkled it with his thumb. It was a picture of a woman, a pretty blonde. We both stared at the picture for a minute in silence.

"Does the woman in the picture look familiar to you?" I asked.

He shook his head. "No, not really. But I think I should hold on to this, just in case." He put the picture in his pocket and then smiled at me.

"Let's go home."

* * * *

Back home, I made some hamburgers for dinner. Danny helped make them, carefully sprinkling his secret seasoning on each of the patties. It was just garlic powder mixed with salt and pepper, but it really did make the best-tasting burgers. Then we all sat out back around the grill while they were cooking.

"Are they almost done?" asked Danny. "I'm starved!"

"Just a few more minutes," I answered. "We don't want to eat them raw." John flipped the burgers one last time, and he looked at Danny. "So, how was that basketball game today?"

Danny shrugged. "It was okay, I guess. Our team won. I don't usually go, but Tommy wanted me to go with him."

John smiled and nodded. "You and Tommy have become close friends, haven't you?"

Danny took a sip of his root beer and wiped his face with the back of his hand. "Yeah, he's my best friend now."

"Well, that's great." John said. "You can never have too many friends." After we had eaten dinner, John and Danny went to do some finishing touches on the tree house, while I cleaned up the kitchen. I was finished and just about to go join them, when I heard the phone ring. I dried my hands with a dish towel before I picked it up.

"Hello?"

"Hello," said a man's voice on the other end. "I'm trying to reach John Doe."

I looked out the window and saw John and Danny laughing as they painted the tree house. They were both covered in blue paint, and I smiled when I saw how happy they both looked.

"He's busy right now," I said. "Can I take a message for him?"

"This is detective Jackson Brown from the Sacramento police department," he said. "I have been working on his case, and we just learned that the car he was driving, the white Mercedes, was registered to a Julie Moore. We are searching for her right now, and hopefully she can shed some light on who he was before the accident. We are investigating the car also, and we should have some answers about that soon. Anyway, if you could pass on the message, and tell him to get back to me at his earliest convenience, I would appreciate it."

I looked through the window again, and my heart sank. Who was this Julie Moore? If she was someone who had been important to John before the accident, then what did that mean for us? I had never felt a connection as strong as the one I felt with John, and I couldn't imagine my life without him now.

"Ma'am, are you still there?" said the voice on the other end.

"Yes," I said, suddenly back in reality. "I will give him the message." After Danny was in bed that night, John and I sat together and watched the last half of an old western film. It was old fashioned and corny, but that's what made it so funny, and we laughed through most of it. When it was over, I grabbed the remote and turned the TV off. We both sat in silence for a few minutes, until John finally spoke.

"We're a talkative bunch," he joked. I nodded, but didn't say anything. I was too busy thinking about my conversation with the police detective. "Is everything all right?" he asked. "You've been quiet tonight."

I paused. "I'm all right. Just a little tired, I guess."

He nodded. "You have a right to be tired. You've had a busy day. Thanks again for taking me to the crash site."

"You're welcome. I'm just sorry we couldn't find more answers."

He shrugged. "Don't worry about it. Who knows, maybe the picture I found will end up being someone who knew me before. I was thinking about calling the news station to see if they might do a segment about it."

I thought again about Julie Moore and how she might be connected to John. I started to tell him about my earlier conversation with the police detective, when he turned and kissed me, and suddenly, nothing else mattered. I thought to myself that I would tell him tomorrow, but I knew deep down that it was a lie. I wanted every moment I could have with him. Right now, he was mine, and I would do anything in my power to keep it that way.

CHAPTER 29

The next couple of days flew by. I still hadn't told John about my conversation with the police detective; it had just never felt like the right time. On Thursday night, he took me to dinner at a new Mexican restaurant. He told me the owners had been at the grocery store, handing out samples, and the food was really good. Danny was having dinner at Tommy's house, so we had the evening to ourselves.

"Everything looks good," John said, looking over his menu. "Yes, it does," I agreed. "But I always love a good enchilada."

John nodded. "Well, why don't we start with some nachos? And a couple of beers?"

"That sounds perfect," I said.

We ordered our food and relaxed for a while, sipping on water while we waited.

"I'm glad you're with me tonight," said John. He put his napkin in his lap and reached across the table to take my hand.

"I'm glad to be here," I said as I squeezed his hand.

He smiled, and then his expression turned more serious. "So, I have something to ask you."

I suddenly felt a little nervous. "What's that?"

"Well, this may sound a little silly. I mean, I know we've been spending a lot of time together. And it's been great, it really has. But I guess what I want to know is, are we exclusive? I know I don't want to see anyone else, so I want to know, do you feel the same way?"

My heart did somersaults in my chest. Since David and I had divorced, I hadn't dated much. I don't think David had ever asked me if we were exclusive, and we probably never were. But something about the way John said it was really sweet, and I could tell he meant every word of it. John and I did have a special connection, and I could see myself with him forever. But I still couldn't forget about my talk with the police detective. As much as I wanted to be with John, maybe he wasn't mine to take. I started to open my mouth, but just then the waitress came up to us.

"I have two beers and a supreme nacho," she said, placing the food and drinks in front of us. "Enjoy." She smiled and walked off to help another table.

I took a drink of my beer and a bite of my nachos. I was trying to buy some time before I answered John's question.

He took a long pull of his beer and smiled at me. "I know what's going on here."

"You do?" I asked, surprised.

He nodded, grabbing a chip from the plate in front of us. "You're scared, and I can't say I blame you. Your marriage ended badly, so I'm sure that makes it hard for you to trust someone. And then I come along, with no history or memory of who I am. I can see why you would hesitate. But something inside me just tells me I'm meant to be here with you."

I nodded. "I feel the same way, but what if it's not enough? What if—" He held up his hand to cut me off. "Why can't that be enough, Jen? Maybe I don't know what the future holds, but I know that right now I'm falling for you. And I really hope you feel the same way about me."

I took a deep breath. "I do."

* * * *

Later that night, I lay awake in my bed, tossing and turning for hours. There were so many thoughts going through my head. I really cared about John, and that was exciting and scary all at the same time. But there was so much about him I didn't know. If his car was registered to Julie Moore, then he had to be connected to her somehow. But how? I got out of bed and wandered out to my computer. I jiggled the mouse and watched it come to life. The screen saver was a picture of Danny and me at the fair a few years ago. His face was painted with tiger stripes, and we both had big smiles on our faces. I clicked on the Internet icon and watched my homepage come on. Then I googled the name Julie Moore. Of course, there were hundreds of results. I scrolled down slowly, not knowing exactly what I was looking for. Then, halfway down the page, I noticed the picture. It was a blonde, and I realized right away it was the same person as in the picture we had found where John's car had crashed. John had planned to take the picture to the news station so they could do a story about it and see if it was someone he knew, but I wasn't sure whether he'd done that yet.

I clicked on the picture, and that took me to a newspaper article. I noticed the date of the article was over five years ago. The title was: "New Jersey Woman Loses Her Husband in Tragic Fire, but Her Positive Attitude Gives Others Hope." I read on.

Julie Dalton may have lost her husband just a few short months ago, but she's already spreading the word about fire safety. Jack Dalton died when their house caught fire in early December, sending the whole community into a state of shock. He was a beloved teacher and football coach at Victory High School and was well liked by everyone who knew him. Julie has been going around to several schools, teaching the importance of fire safety. Although the exact cause of the fire is unknown, it is thought to have started when a candle was left unattended. Julie wants to educate everyone she can about fire safety. "If I can just save one life, it will be worth it," she says.

I took a deep breath and looked at the picture again. There was no doubt it was the same woman from the photo John and I had found a few days earlier. Julie was handing out flyers to people, with a big smile on her face. She looked so sweet, and my heart really went out to her. It must have been so traumatic to lose her husband like that. But it still didn't answer the big question I had: How was she connected to John? I sighed before I turned off my computer and went to bed.

CHAPTER 30

The next day was Friday, and I was excited to start my weekend. It had been a long week, full of so many different emotions, and that can be draining sometimes. It was Danny's weekend at his dad's house, and I was sure he would have that pitiful puppy-dog look he always had when he had to go there. I wasn't sure if I really wanted him to go anyway, after the way David had talked to me the last time. I still hadn't heard anything from his lawyer, and I knew him well enough to know he was full of hot air. All talk and no action. Still, it really upset me that he would make threats like that. Just thinking about it made me feel like hitting something.

I was surprised when I pulled up at Danny's school and saw him waiting for me with a big smile on his face. He walked up to the car slowly, and that's when I noticed he seemed a little out of breath.

"Hi, Mom."

"Hi, Danny, how was your day?"

"Fine," he said.

I looked at him a little closer and noticed how pale he looked. His lips looked a little blue, too. I thought to myself that he had been a little more tired than usual lately. He'd gone to bed early every night that week. "Are you feeling okay?" I touched his forehead to feel for a fever, just as all moms instinctively do.

"I'm fine, Mom. We had to run the track at PE today, that's all."

I nodded. "Okay. You know if you aren't feeling up to it, you don't have to go to your dad's house this weekend. We can just call him and tell him you're sick."

"What? No, I want to go."

My jaw dropped. "You want to go to your dad's house?"

He nodded. "It's Max's birthday, and we're going to Golfland. You know how much I love to miniature golf."

"Yes," I said. "I didn't realize there was something special going on." I looked him over suspiciously. "Are you sure you're all right?"

"I'm fine, Mom. Stop worrying so much!"

"I'll always worry about you," I said. "That's my job. Just promise you'll call me if you need anything."

"I will."

* * * *

When the doorbell rang just a little while later, Danny had his bag packed and was waiting by the window. I took a deep breath as I went to answer the door. I felt a little uneasy about him going to David's house, but at the same time, it was rare that he actually wanted to go to his dad's. And even if David was the biggest jerk on the planet, he was still Danny's dad. Danny deserved to know his father. When I opened the door, David stood there with that same smirk he always wore, and I had to fight the urge to slam the door in his face.

"Hi, Jen. Is Danny all ready to go?"

Danny ran up behind me. "I'm all packed. I just forgot one thing; I'll be right back."

Danny ran upstairs to his room, and I turned to David. "Listen, I don't think Danny's feeling very well. He looks a little pale to me."

David rolled his eyes. "Why do you waste so much time trying to find something wrong with him? You really need to stop smothering him."

I crossed my arms over my chest and narrowed my eyes at him. "How dare you! I'm just being a concerned mom, and I thought you should know this, since he'll be with you for the next couple of days."

Just then, Danny came running downstairs with his camera case over his shoulder. I'd given him the camera for his last birthday, and he loved taking pictures with it. "I'm all ready to go." He looked at David and back at me. "Is everything all right?"

David looked at him with that phony smile of his. "Everything is peachy keen, son. Can you go wait in the car? I'll be right there."

"Okay. Bye, Mom." Danny came up and gave me quick hug and kiss before he walked out to the car.

David turned to me, and cleared his throat. "Listen, Jen, I wanted to talk to you about this whole custody issue again. I'm moving in September, and I was hoping we could settle it out of court. I really don't want to put Danny through a long ordeal, but—"

"There's nothing to discuss," I cut him off. "Danny stays with me, end of discussion. I didn't even want him to go with you this weekend."

He shook his head and laughed. "So the truth comes out. You just wanted Danny to be sick so he'd stay with you this weekend. Now who's being selfish? What's wrong, are you lonely? Is there trouble with the mystery man?"

I smiled. "No trouble at all. He's ten times the man you'll ever be. Much better in bed, too."

David sighed. "Whatever. So I guess I'll be seeing you in court."

"See you there," I said as I slammed to door in his face.

CHAPTER 31

When I woke up the next morning, I started cleaning my house from top to bottom. I always cleaned when I was mad about something; it was a great stress release. I couldn't stop thinking about what David had said. I couldn't for the life of me figure out what I ever saw in that jerk. He didn't really want Danny; he just wanted to get under my skin. And it was working. I think that was the part that bothered me most of all. Why did I let him have so much power over me?

I had already scrubbed all of the baseboards and cleaned both bathrooms, when there was a knock on the back door. I let out a big sigh. I was normally excited to see John, but right now, I wasn't really in the mood to be around anyone. Don't get me wrong, I missed him whenever he wasn't with me. I hadn't seen him at all yesterday, since he'd worked overtime at the grocery store. I looked down at my bleach-stained clothes and peeked at my reflection in the mirror one last time before I went to open the door.

"Good morning," he said, looking as handsome as ever. He looked around the house with a curious expression on his face. "Doing a little cleaning?"

I nodded. "This is my version of venting about my ex-husband."

"Does it work?"

I laughed. "Not really. And I must look like a mess."

"You look beautiful," he said, meaning it. Then he pulled me close to him and kissed me.

"Now, that just might work," I said. "I feel better already."

He smiled. "Good. Listen, there's a concert going on at the park down the street today. It's an eighties tribute band, and I thought it would be something fun for us to do. Do you want to go?"

I looked down at my clothes again. "Okay, just give me an hour or so to freshen up."

I showered, changed, and put on some makeup. When I looked in the mirror, I was pleased with what I saw. My wavy hair fell neatly to my shoulders, and I was wearing a crisp blue T-shirt with some denim shorts. It

was such a big improvement from how I had looked before, with my hair such a mess, in my old tattered clothes. It's amazing what a shower and a little makeup can do.

When I was ready, I went out to the guest house to get John. It seemed that he had been waiting for me, because he answered the door just as soon as I knocked.

He looked me up and down, with a smile on his face. "You look amazing. But then again, that's nothing new. You always look nice."

"Oh, stop it," I said playfully.

He laughed. "You really should learn to take a compliment."

I nodded. "I'll try. I guess it's just easier to believe the negative stuff."

He shrugged. "Well, get used to hearing the positive stuff, because that's all you're going to be hearing from me."

I smiled, and looked around the little guest house. I noticed he had done a lot of work around the place. The living room had a fresh coat of paint, and all the holes in the walls had been repaired. My heart almost stopped when I noticed there was a huge picture hanging on the living room wall. It was John and me the day we'd gone to San Francisco. The

Golden Gate Bridge was behind us, and we both had huge smiles on our faces. I had almost forgotten that I'd brought my camera that day.

"Wow," I said. "You've really done a lot around here."

He followed my gaze to the picture. "I had that done at the photo center at work. I hope you don't mind. It was such a great picture of the two of us; I just couldn't resist."

I smiled. "I don't mind at all." I looked around and noticed there were also some photos of the three of us in small frames sitting on an end table. Something about that small gesture just made my heart melt. It showed that John considered Danny and me to be his family. It also made me feel bad because I didn't have any pictures of us up at my place.

"Well," he said, "are you ready to go?"

I reached out and took his hand. "I'm ready to go anywhere, as long as you're there."

He beamed, and we walked to the park together, laughing, talking, and holding hands.

When we got there, people were scattered all over the grass. Children were running around, kicking balls and blowing bubbles. Someone was grilling food on a huge barbecue, and there was a jump house set up at the far end of the park. There were even vendors set up with ice cream and cotton candy, and a mixture of scents filled the air. I thought to myself that Danny would have loved it there, and I wondered how he was doing at his dad's house. But I was glad to have this time with John, and I wanted to enjoy every minute.

"There's a spot right over there," I said. "We can spread out our blanket on the grass, and we should be able to get a pretty good view of the concert."

He nodded, and we both walked over and laid out the blanket I'd brought. It was an old quilt my grandmother had given me years ago, and I always thought of her whenever I used it. We both sat down on the blanket, leaning into each other and getting comfortable.

"This is perfect," he said. "I saw this band on TV, and they're really good, so we're in for a treat."

"Well, thanks for inviting me," I said. "If it weren't for you, I probably would have spent the day cleaning."

He shook his head. "That wouldn't be any fun at all."

"No, it wouldn't." We both sat silently for a minute, and then John's expression turned more serious.

"So, your ex still wants custody of Danny?"

I nodded. "At least that's what he says. My dad gave me a business card for an old lawyer friend of his, so I'm going to call him Monday. If David wants a fight, that's exactly what he's going to get. There's no way I'm letting him take Danny anywhere."

Just then the band came out, and everyone cheered. They started with the song "Take on Me," which was one of my favorites. I could still remember the video on MTV, and I sang along. I looked over at John, who was singing, too; he knew all the lyrics. I wondered whether he somehow remembered the song or whether he just knew it because he had seen the band on TV. I wondered how much of him was Derek from before the accident, and how much of him was the John I knew. There were probably bits and pieces of his earlier life stored in there somewhere, so deep he couldn't remember. But I decided not to overanalyze it. To me he was John, the man who had my heart. We danced together and listened to the music for the rest of the afternoon, without a care in the world.

* * * *

When we got home that evening, we bounced into the house, laughing, and singing some of the songs we'd heard at the concert. We both flopped down on the couch together, melting into each other and enjoying the moment. We kissed, and it was probably one of the most passionate kisses I'd had in my life. We were both really into it, but then I started thinking about my talk with the police detective and about Julie Moore.

"Hey, John, there's something we should talk about." He sighed. "I'm not really in the mood for talking."

"I know," I said. "But this is important."

"All right. As long as we can continue this after we talk."

I started to open my mouth, when the phone rang. I would have just let the machine pick it up, but then I thought that it might be Danny. I knew he wasn't feeling well, and I'd told him to call me if he wanted to come home.

"I really should answer that," I said with a sigh. And I walked over and picked up the phone. "Hello?"

There was a pause before a weak voice came on the other line.

"Hi, Jen." It was David. I was surprised to hear his voice, since he never called me.

"Hi, David. Is something wrong?"

It sounded like he was crying on the other end. "I need you to come to the hospital as soon as you can. It's Danny."

CHAPTER 32

When John and I arrived at the hospital just a few minutes later, it seemed to take forever to find a parking place. Then the elevators were all out of order, so we frantically ran upstairs to pediatrics. When we finally got there, we saw David sitting in the waiting room, with his face buried in his hands. It looked as if he had been crying, but I wasn't worried about him. I was more concerned about Danny.

"What happened?" I exclaimed as I sat in a chair across from him. John sat down quietly beside me.

David looked up, with a tear-streaked face. His voice was hoarse, as if he had been crying for a while. In all of the years I'd known him, I'd never seen him cry, and that just made me worry even more.

"We were at the park, playing baseball," he began. "Max has a big game, so we were practicing. Then Danny said he wanted to play, too. He hit the ball so far, it flew out of the park. I was so proud of him. Then, just as he was coming to third base, he collapsed. He was unresponsive at first, and that's when I called the ambulance. He started talking again, but he's so weak."

"Where is he?" I demanded.

"They took him back to run some tests," he answered. "They said they would let us know when they're done."

In that moment, I did what I had wanted to do for years. It happened so suddenly, I almost couldn't believe it myself. I threw back my hand and slapped David right across the face. I hit him so hard there was a red mark across his cheek. He held his hand to his cheek, and then he slowly looked up at me.

"I deserved that," was all that he could say.

"You bet you deserved that!" I yelled. "I told you Danny wasn't feeling well, and you let him play baseball? It's nearly one hundred degrees outside! Have you ever heard of heat stroke?"

He nodded. "Well, just so you know, seeing him like that was a big wake-up call for me. It made me realize you know him a lot better than I do. You were right—he belongs with you. I'm not going to try to take Danny with me to New York. But I do hope he can come visit me sometimes."

"We'll talk about that later," I said.

Just then, a doctor came into the waiting room. He looked familiar, and I recognized him as the head doctor in pediatrics. I'd heard some really good things about him, so I was glad he was taking care of Danny. "I'm looking for the parents of Daniel Morrison," he said.

David and I both stood up and walked toward him, and I noticed John sinking into his seat. I felt horrible when I realized I hadn't even introduced him to David. I had been so wrapped up in the moment I'd almost forgotten he was there. I grabbed his hand, and he followed us to where the doctor was standing. I knew that in the short time John had known us, he had come to care about Danny a lot, and he'd want to hear what the doctor had to say. "I'm Doctor Rogers," He introduced himself and shook everyone's hand.

"You must be Mom and Dad?" He looked at John and me curiously.

"No, this is Danny's father." I gestured toward David. "And this is my friend, John."

"Okay, well, it's nice to meet all of you. I'm sure you're wondering how Danny is doing, so I'll just cut to the chase. We've run a variety of tests, including an echocardiogram, and it looks like Danny has an atrial septal defect, a hole between the two upper chambers of his heart. Has anyone ever noticed a heart murmur when he's gone in for routine checkups?"

I took a deep breath. "No, or if they did, they didn't tell me about it. How could I not know Danny has a heart defect?"

He put his hand on my shoulder sympathetically. "Don't blame yourself. Most of the time, these kind of defects are caught at birth, or shortly after. But sometimes the murmur just isn't noticeable, especially if the doctor is distracted or if there is a lot of noise in the room."

I nodded. When Danny was younger, he'd hated going to the doctor, and he would cry and whine the entire time. That would be enough to distract even the most patient doctor.

"So, what do we do next?" I asked.

Doctor Rogers pursed his lips together, as if deep in thought. "Well, the shunt is significant enough that it should be surgically repaired. Luckily, we have one of the best pediatric cardiologists on staff right here. Doctor Carson will be reviewing his file, and we will get him scheduled for surgery."

I felt all of the blood drain from my face. The thought of Danny lying on the surgery table, with some strange man's hands in his chest was more than I could handle.

"Are you sure he needs surgery?" I asked quietly.

He nodded. "If we don't correct this now, he's at risk for a lot of medical issues. Hypertension, stroke, and heart failure, just to name a few. I know open-heart surgery is a scary thing, but advances in medical technology have made this a relatively low-risk procedure."

I felt a little lightheaded, and I leaned against John for a moment to get my balance. He put his arm around me, which was just what I needed to regain my composure. "Can I see him?" I asked.

The doctor nodded. "He's been asking for you. Just make your visit brief; he does need to rest."

* * * *

Danny's room seemed too white and sterile, and he looked so small lying in the hospital bed. I thought he was sleeping at first, but as soon as I came closer to him, his eyes fluttered open, and he looked right at me.

"Hi, Mom."

"Hi, baby. How are you feeling?"

"Okay," he said. "A little tired. Did they find out what's wrong with me?"

I thought about all of the symptoms he'd had recently—the blue lips, being tired all the time and out of breath. *I'm a nurse for crying out loud! How could I not notice my own son had a heart defect?*

"Yes," I said. "And they're going to fix it."

He considered this for a minute. "Will I need surgery?"

I nodded and brushed his hair away from his face. "But they have the best doctors here, and they are going to take such good care of you."

He smiled. "Cool." Then he paused for a moment before he continued, "You should have seen me hit that ball, Mom. It would have been a home run. You would have been so proud of me."

I felt the tears start to run down my face. "I know I would have, sweetie." He looked around curiously. "Is John here?"

I nodded. "He's out in the waiting room."

"Can I see him?"

I wiped the tears out of my eyes and let out a big sigh of relief. I had a feeling Danny was going to be just fine.

CHAPTER 33

The next couple of days felt like a blur. Danny stayed in the hospital for observation. He had shortness of breath and heart palpitations, symptoms the doctor promised would cease after his surgery. His surgery was scheduled for Tuesday morning, and he would probably be staying for a couple of days after that. Working at the hospital did have its advantages. They were very understanding when I told them I needed some time off to take care of Danny. I also had my own cot in Danny's room, something they didn't give to everyone. I only went home to shower and get some things that would make Danny and me more comfortable during our stay there. I brought him some extra clothes, some books, and his handheld video game. I brought myself some extra clothes, some makeup, and some snacks for the two of us to share. I'd never been a big fan of hospital food.

Spending so much time on the pediatrics floor reminded me why I had decided not to specialize in peds. There was a lot of crying, and the parents were always watching every move the doctors and nurses made. I never worked well under that kind of pressure. And the thought of having such young lives in my hands was just too much for me to handle.

Danny had a roommate, a six-year-old boy named Garret. He had many health problems, including kidney failure, and he was going to get a new kidney on the same day Danny was having his surgery. The two boys had become fast friends, but I thought it was a little sad that I had only seen his mother once, and no other family members came to visit him. The mother seemed nice, but I got the feeling she was at the end of her rope. It must have been hard to raise a kid with so many problems.

On Sunday night, John brought a pizza for dinner. I was relieved to be eating something besides hospital food, and Danny looked as if he might just do cartwheels right there in his hospital bed.

"Thanks, John!"

"You're welcome," he said. "I thought you might enjoy this, especially since you won't be eating much after tomorrow."

Danny rolled his eyes. "Don't remind me."

I passed out some paper plates, and we all started eating like starving dogs. Then we looked over at little Garret, who was staring at our pizza longingly.

"Would you like some?" I asked.

He nodded, and a big smile swept over his face.

We all ate together, laughing and talking as we did. I thought again how lucky I was. Maybe Danny was sick, but he could be fixed. And I felt so lucky to have John in my life. He was thoughtful and caring, and I knew he thought the world of Danny and me. Once again, he had helped me get through a time that would have been so much more difficult without him. He'd given me hope that maybe my happily-ever-after was possible after all.

CHAPTER

34

On Tuesday morning, I was a nervous wreck. Although I had met Danny's surgeon and researched his credentials, I knew that open-heart surgery was a big deal. Danny would be put on a heart-lung machine while the doctor closed the hole in his heart. David had taken the day off work, so he could wait with me during Danny's surgery. I was amazed at how much he had changed since the day Danny collapsed on the baseball field. I guess that was one good thing that had come out of Danny's heart condition. Maybe now he would have a better relationship with his father.

John had to work a half day at the grocery store, but he would be coming to the hospital as soon as he was done. I couldn't wait to get this over with and have Danny back home, where he belonged.

David and I each sat on one side of Danny's bed while we waited for the surgeon to arrive. Danny hadn't been able to eat anything since the day before, and he was starving.

"Do you think after the surgery I can have a great, big, juicy cheeseburger?" he asked, breaking the silence.

"We'll just have to wait and see what the doctor says," I told him.

He sighed. "Is he going to be here soon? I really want to get this over with."

"Me too," I said. "We just have to be patient."

Danny looked over at David, who hadn't said more than two words since he got there. "Don't worry, Dad. I'm going to be just fine."

"I know you are, son," he said. "You're the strongest kid I know."

Just then Doctor Carson entered the room. A nurse followed behind him, pushing a gurney. "Hello, everybody," he said. "How are we doing today?"

Danny smiled. "Besides the hole in my heart, I'm just fine."

Doctor Carson laughed and playfully ruffled Danny's hair. "Well, we are going to fix that. Is everyone familiar with the procedure?"

Danny and I both nodded; he'd already gone over it with us the day before when he came to visit. But David just sat there. The doctor sensed that David was upset, and he put a hand on his shoulder.

"Don't worry, I've repaired so many ASD holes, I can almost do it in my sleep."

David's eyes widened; he obviously didn't think that was funny.

Doctor Carson cleared his throat. "Don't worry; I wouldn't actually do the surgery in my sleep. We're just going to make an incision in Danny's chest. Then I will sew a patch of surgical material over the hole. I will close him back up, and in six months or so, the hole will be covered with tissue. He should make a quick recovery and be back to his old self before you know it."

David nodded. "Just take good care of my boy."

"Don't worry," the doctor said. "He's in good hands. Okay, are we ready to go?"

Danny nodded. "I just want to get this over with."

The nurse pushed the gurney closer to Danny's bed, and he scooted from the bed to the gurney. David and I followed him as far as the waiting room, where we would have to say our good-byes.

"I'll see you when I wake up," said Danny, smiling.

I gave him a hug and a kiss on the cheek. "Do you know how proud I am of you?" I said, and Danny beamed.

Then David hugged Danny and kissed him on the cheek. That surprised me, since he usually wasn't a very affectionate man.

"I love you, son."

"Love you, too, Dad."

With that, they pushed Danny through the double doors that led to the OR and David and I sat down in the waiting room. I knew that this was going to be the longest wait of my life.

CHAPTER 35

Time seemed to stand still while Danny was in surgery. David and I each sat there silently, pretending to look at some old magazines. Finally, he broke the silence.

"I know I've never told you this, but Danny is really lucky to have you for his mother."

"Thanks," I said. "That means a lot coming from you. But I have to tell you something."

"What's that?"

"I'm not sorry I slapped you. You've really been a jerk."

He laughed. "Fair enough." Then he paused, deep in thought. "I just want us to come to some sort of understanding, for Danny's sake."

I nodded. "We can agree to disagree."

"I can live with that," he said.

We went back to our magazines, just as John walked into the waiting room. He looked out of breath, as if he'd run all the way there. "Any word yet?"

I shook my head. "Nope. They took him in about half an hour ago, but it feels like hours already." I patted the spot next to me, and he came to sit down. Then he looked over at David.

"How are you doing?"

"As well as I can under the circumstances," he answered. "Listen, I want you both to know how sorry I am. I know I've behaved like a jackass, and I'm trying really hard to be a better person. I can see that the two of you make each other happy, and Danny has only good things to say about you." He looked at John and continued, "Thanks for being the father figure in his life when I wasn't. I was so wrapped up in myself, I forgot to put my son first, and I regret that. And Jen, I really hope you'll at least consider letting Danny visit me in New York."

I sighed. "I'll think about it. Let's just worry about getting him well first."

The three of us waited in awkward silence. It seemed like days before doctor Carson finally emerged from behind the doors. The three of us stood up and walked toward him. I tried to read his expression, but it was neutral, somewhere between happy and depressed. Then he looked at us and smiled.

"The surgery went well. Danny's in recovery, and you'll be able to see him shortly."

All three of us let out huge sighs of relief. I looked at the doctor and smiled. "Thank you," I told him.

* * * *

When I entered Danny's room, he was sleeping peacefully in his bed. He looked pale and weak and he was hooked up to a bunch of tubes and machines. My heart sank when I saw him like that and I realized I would take his place in a heartbeat. I sat in the chair beside his bed and took his hand.

"You are probably the bravest kid I know" I said to him. "You came through that surgery with flying colors, but that doesn't surprise me. I bet you will be back to your old self before you know it. Then you can brag to all of your friends about the cool patch on your heart. But right now, I just want you to get some rest and concentrate on getting better, okay?" I kissed him on the forehead and tucked him in before I walked out of the room.

After we had all had a chance to see Danny, David had to go back to work. He said he'd gotten really behind since Danny got sick, and he had a lot to do to get ready for the move. John and I went down to the cafeteria to get a bite to eat. The food wasn't that great, but neither of us had eaten all day, so I was sure it would taste like a five-star meal.

"Danny looks great," John said as we sat down at our table, sipping our Cokes.

"Yes, he does," I agreed. "I think he will make a speedy recovery." John nodded in agreement. "He's lucky to have a mom like you."

"Thanks," I said. "You know, David said exactly the same thing."

He looked surprised. "Wow, he really has changed." He looked around the cafeteria, and then he took a bite of his roast beef sandwich. "Do you ever think about going back with him?" he asked.

"No," I said quickly. "David might be acting a little bit nicer lately, but that doesn't mean we were meant to be together. There's a reason things didn't work out between us." I smiled and took his hand. "Besides, I already have the greatest man in my life, who makes me very happy."

He raised an eyebrow. "Really? Can I meet this guy, because I'd like to punch his lights out for trying to steal my girlfriend." We both laughed, and we gazed into each other's eyes. Then John squeezed my hand. "Hey, Jen?"

"Yes?"

"Wasn't there something you wanted to tell me, before you got the phone call about Danny?"

I nodded and started to open my mouth. But just as I started to speak, Lisa walked up to our table.

"Hi, guys. How's Danny?"

"He's doing great," I said. "The surgery went well, and he should be able to come home in a couple of days."

She smiled. "That's great news. Listen, I'm glad I ran into you, because time cards are due. They are going to collect them in about twenty minutes, so if you want to get paid, you should fill yours out."

I nodded. "Thank you, Lisa; I will do that right now." I looked at John. "I'll be right back."

I took the elevator up to the second floor, and went into the little cubicle where our time sheets were kept. I took it out to the nurses' station and rummaged around in the drawer to find a pen. Then I heard someone walk up to the nurses' station.

"Excuse me," I heard a woman's voice say. "I'm looking for someone, and I was hoping you could help me."

"Oh, I'm not on duty," I answered without looking up. "I think Tina is on duty. I can get her to help you just as soon as I'm done with this."

It was then that the woman started to cry, and I finally looked up at her and realized who she was. It was the woman from the photo we'd found at the crash site. The same woman who John's car was registered to. Julie Moore. "I'm just looking for a patient who was in here a few weeks ago with a head injury," she said through her tears. Then she pulled a crumpled picture out of her pocket and set it down on the desk. It was John. In the photo, he was standing in front of a Christmas tree, with a big grin on his face. "Do you recognize him?"

I stood there in stunned silence. "How do you know him?" I managed to say.

She sniffed back her tears and wiped her face with a tissue. "I'm his wife," she said, and then she smiled. "You do know where he is, don't you? Can you take me to him? I've been looking everywhere."

I suddenly felt dizzy, as if all the blood were draining from my face. And I swear my heart stopped beating when I looked down and realized she was at least eight months pregnant.

CHAPTER 36

I stood there, staring at Julie, and part of me wanted to tell her I had never seen that man in my life. I wanted her to go away and leave John and me alone, even if it was only for a little while longer. But deep down, I had known for a while that this day was coming. Sure, I wanted to live in my fantasy world where John, Danny, and I were the only people who mattered. But I knew now that it just wasn't possible. He had a wife, and a baby on the way. Of course, a man as handsome and kind and funny as John wouldn't be single. Good girls like me were destined to be alone. As much as I wanted to make her go away, I knew I had to do the right thing.

"He's down in the cafeteria," I said in an almost-whisper. "Follow me." I led the way, and she followed.

"Thank you so much! You don't know how much this means to me," she said. "I've been in Europe, visiting family. I didn't know anything about the accident. But I have been trying to get hold of Derek, and my messages were going straight to his voice mail. I finally came home early, because I just knew something was wrong. That's when I saw him on the news. They said he has amnesia?"

I nodded and tried my best to fight the tears that were forming in my eyes.

"So, does he still have it?" she asked.

"Have what?" I rubbed my eyes, knowing I was smearing my mascara. "Amnesia. I mean, he doesn't remember anything from before the accident, right?" She stopped for a moment, looking at a picture on the wall.

Something about the way she asked seemed strange to me. It was almost as if she didn't want him to remember. "That's right," I said. "He can't remember anything from before, not yet."

I swear she let out a sigh of relief.

"Well, the cafeteria is right through these doors," I said. "He's in here. I think it would probably be best if I went and told him you're coming first. That way it won't be such a shock."

She nodded. "I think that's a great idea. Oh, and I never asked you what your name is."

"Jennifer. My friends call me Jen."

"And how did you know Derek?"

"I was his nurse," I answered.

She nodded and said, "Well, thanks for taking care of my husband when I wasn't there." She rubbed her stomach, and that was enough to make the tears start rolling down my face. But I turned around and walked into the cafeteria before she noticed.

John was still sitting at the table we'd been sharing just a few minutes ago, but somehow, now it all seemed like a dream. When he saw me, he looked up and smiled. "Hey, you."

I smiled a weak little smile and walked over to him. He must have noticed something was wrong, because he stood up and started walking toward me. "Are you okay? Did something happen with Danny?"

I shook my head. "No. But there's someone here who wants to see you."

He looked surprised. "Who?"

"Your wife."

His jaw dropped. "I have a wife?"

I nodded. "She's the woman you found a picture of in the bushes where your car crashed. Her name is Julie."

He seemed deep in thought. "That name just doesn't ring a bell. How come she didn't try to find me before?"

"She says she was in Europe, visiting family," I answered.

John rubbed his temples, as if he were trying to will himself to remember something. "It just doesn't make sense."

"Well, maybe it will make more sense when you meet her," I said.

As I turned and walked to the door, I knew there was no turning back. Things would be forever changed between John and me. I opened the door and motioned for Julie to come in. As soon as she saw John, she threw her arms around him, hugging him tight.

"Oh, Derek, I've missed you so much!"

I decided it would be best to give them some time alone, so I walked out of the cafeteria and straight across the hall to the bathroom. And that's when I finally lost it. I locked myself in one of the stalls, and I stood there, bawling like a baby.

CHAPTER

37

It's amazing how quickly life can change. Just three days ago, I hadn't known Danny had a heart defect. I'd been at a concert with John, without a care in the world. I hadn't known John for very long, but I was starting to think about what a future with him might look like—the three of us, spending time together, like a family. Maybe we'd even get married. Now that I'd finally found someone who I felt a real connection with, someone that I could really see a future with, it turned out he was married to someone else. What had I been thinking, anyway? I had been crazy to start planning a future with someone who couldn't remember who he was. I had set myself up for major heartbreak.

After I had cried enough tears to fill a river, I washed my face in the sink and looked at my reflection. My eyes were still a little red and puffy; that was to be expected. But I still looked a lot better than I had a few minutes ago. And I knew the one thing that would make everything all right again. I needed to see Danny. I took the elevator to the third floor and turned right down the hall, to room 326. His room was quiet, except for the sound of his monitors beeping. I sat in the chair beside his bed, and his eyes fluttered open. He looked up at me with a weak little smile.

"Hey, baby. How are you doing?" I asked.

"Okay, I guess. Did they fix me?" He asked in a weak voice.

"Yes, you're as good as new."

I scooted closer to him. I put my arm around him, and we snuggled like that for a few minutes.

"I can't wait to go home," he said with a sigh.

I smiled. "I can't wait to bring you home. Just a couple more days, I promise."

"Good," he said, "because John promised to help me build some shelves in the tree house, for my books and things. And Tommy's birthday party is coming up; I can't miss that."

I felt the tears start to puddle up again. What was I going to tell Danny? He had really bonded with John; I knew he would take it hard. But I didn't want him to worry about anything except getting well, so I just smiled and nodded. After all, there was no need to make him worry, when even I didn't know how this whole thing would end.

"Mom, is everything okay?" Danny had always been perceptive about people's feelings. He knew when I was sad, even if I tried my best to hide it. I wrapped my arms around him and hugged him tight.

"Everything's just fine, son."

Then I felt him look over my shoulder, toward the doorway. "Hi, John." I turned around to see John standing there. He smiled at Danny, but I could see the worry and fear in his eyes.

"Hi, buddy. How are you doing?"

"Okay, but hospitals are boring. I can't wait to get home and work on the tree house." There was an awkward silence, and then a worried look came over Danny's face. "We are still going to work on the shelves, aren't we?"

"I'll try my best." John answered, and that seemed to satisfy Danny, for the moment. "Listen, can I borrow your mom for a minute? I want to talk to her about something."

Danny nodded. "Sure, go ahead."

John motioned for me to come with him, so I followed him out to the hallway. I looked around, trying to spot Julie, but she was nowhere to be seen. As soon as we were out of Danny's earshot, John took a deep breath. Nobody else was around; it was just the two of us.

"I don't know how to say this," he blurted out. "I don't think I've ever been so confused."

We both sat down in some chairs that were lined up against the wall.

Then John put his face in his hands, deep in thought.

I put my hand on his shoulder. "It's okay. Whatever you need to do, I understand."

"You're so sweet," he said quietly. "That only makes this harder. I mean, I don't know her, but I care about you so much. All of my memories right now have you and Danny in them. And all of my dreams for the future do, too. But now this woman comes to me and tells me that we were married, that we are expecting a child together, and I don't remember her at all." He paused for a minute. "I don't know what to do."

I nodded. "I want you to do whatever is best for you."

"And that's just it; I don't know what's best for me right now," he said.

Then he took me in his arms and squeezed me tight. We were both crying.

"Well," I finally managed through my tears, "I think you and I both knew this was coming sometime."

He shook his head. "I didn't. I mean, I thought that if someone was going to come back for me, they would have done it by now. And I wasn't even wearing a wedding ring. What kind of husband takes off his wedding ring?"

I shrugged, and we both sat there quietly, until John broke the silence. "She wants me to come and stay with her, at our old place. She thinks it might help me remember."

I nodded. "You should go. Maybe it will answer all of the unanswered questions you have about your life." I hated myself as soon as those words came out of my mouth. I really wanted to beg him to stay with me forever, but I knew that just wasn't realistic. Not anymore.

"Will you be okay?" he asked, his voice cracking a little bit. "Sure, I'll be fine," I lied. "I am one tough lady, remember?"

He smiled. "How could I forget?" Then he put his hand on my shoulder. "I'll go by and get my things, and I'll leave the key in the mailbox, okay? Tell Danny I'll try to come over sometime soon and help him with those shelves in his tree house. I just need time to figure out a few things first." He stood up and started to walk away. Then he turned around again. "And, Jen?"

I looked up at him, trying my best to fight the tears. "Yes?"

"No matter what, I won't forget you, and I sure hope you don't forget about me."

With those words, he turned around and walked away, and I was left sitting there, alone.

CHAPTER 38

On Thursday morning, I helped Danny gather his things to go home. Doctor Carson came in to do one more quick checkup before he released him, although Danny had so far passed all the tests with flying colors.

"Your heart sounds great," he said as he listened to Danny's heartbeat with a stethoscope. Then he put the stethoscope back around his neck and looked at me. "So, Mom, I assume you know all of the danger signs to look out for? Signs of infection and so forth?"

I nodded. "Yes. I've done lots of research about ASDs since Danny was brought here. Plus, I'm a nurse, so that helps."

He smiled and winked at me. "I can tell he's in good hands. I'll go get the paperwork ready, so the two of you can get out of here. He reached into his pocket and pulled out a piece of paper. "And maybe while you're waiting, you can go and pick up his medication at the pharmacy." He handed me the paper, and I tucked it into my pocket.

"Sure."

Then he smiled at Danny and playfully ruffled his hair. "You've been a great patient, but I hope I don't see you in here anytime soon."

Danny laughed. "I hope so too."

Doctor Carson walked out of the room, and I sat next to Danny on his bed. "I bet it will feel good to be back in your own bed tonight."

He nodded. "I can't wait to be home." Then he looked at me with a serious expression across his face. "Hey, Mom?"

"What?"

"Do you know how Garret is doing? I haven't seen him since he went in for his surgery. I'd like to say good-bye to him before I go."

I smiled. "I will go find out right now. Then I'll go down to the pharmacy to get your medicine."

I walked out to the nurses' station, where two nurses sat, filling out paperwork. One was a blonde and one was a brunette, and they both looked tired and stressed. I could relate, because I had those days at work sometimes, too.

"Excuse me," I said.

One of the nurses looked up at me. "Can I help you?"

"My son Danny had a roommate when he was admitted here. He was a little boy named Garret. I wondered if you know how he's doing. If it's possible, Danny would like to say good-bye to him before he goes home today."

The nurse looked down and shook her head. "I'm afraid that isn't possible. Garret passed away this morning. There were complications after his surgery, and his little body just wasn't strong enough. It was really sad."

I felt like the air had been sucked right out of my lungs. I remembered his sweet little smile and how tiny and helpless he had been. I looked over to the waiting room, and I saw Garret's mother sitting there, crying. I knew it would have been the right thing to go and comfort her, but I didn't know what to say. My son was coming home, and she would never get to bring Garret home. Besides, I had enough on my plate to deal with right now.

"Thank you," I said to the nurse. And I walked to the elevators and got on without another word.

CHAPTER 39

"We're home!" I said when Danny and I arrived back at the house a little while later. He walked in, and we both looked around. It felt as if I hadn't been home in months, even though it had only been a few days. So much had happened in such a short period of time, and I had so many thoughts going through my head all at once. Danny walked in with his head hanging down, and I realized he hadn't said anything on the way home. The news of Garret's death had really affected him.

"Are you okay?" I asked.

"Yeah, I guess." He looked down at his feet. "It just isn't fair. Garret was three years younger than me. How come he had to die, Mom?"

I took a deep breath. "I don't know, son. I guess some things in life just aren't fair." I was talking about Garret, but I was thinking about John.

"Do you think it was the pizza we gave him?"

"No, I don't think it had anything to do with that. He was just really sick."

Then Danny perked up. "I'm going to tell John I'm home; he'll be so happy!"

He ran out the back door, toward the guest house, before I had the chance to say anything. I hadn't told Danny that John wouldn't be staying with us anymore. I hadn't wanted to upset him while he was sick. And now, I didn't know what to say. I followed him out to the guest house. He was knocking on the door, and I felt on the verge of tears again.

"I don't think John is home," I said.

"When will he be home?"

I shook my head. "He won't."

He looked puzzled. "Why not?"

I knelt down to his level and put my hands on his shoulders. "When you were in the hospital, John's wife came back. He is going to be staying with her for a while. He needs to try to remember who he was before. But he promised he would try to come help you build the shelves in your tree house just as soon as he can."

Danny stood there in silence for a minute, trying to take this all in. "You mean he's not coming back to live with us?"

I sighed. "Probably not."

"But I really like John."

"I know you do, son."

It was then that the tears started rolling down his cheeks. "It's not fair!" He walked across the yard to his tree house, climbed up, and closed himself inside. Then my own tears started to come, slowly at first, and then like a waterfall streaming down my face. I had always promised myself I wouldn't let Danny get so attached to someone who would then be ripped out of his life. What kind of mother was I? I should have known better! I had brought John back to stay in our guest house, introduced him to my son and, worst of all, had allowed myself to fall in love with him. I decided it would be best to give Danny some space for a while, so I went to my own room and cried until I was sure there were no more tears left. I knew I had to pull myself together, for Danny's sake as well as my own.

* * * *

That night, I made tacos for dinner, in an attempt to cheer up Danny. He hadn't come down from his tree house. He probably felt a connection to John while he was in there, since they had built it together. I made two plates and carried them out to the tree house. Danny sat on the floor, pushing a toy car around.

"Hey, sweetie, I made tacos for dinner." I set the plates down before I climbed all the way in and sat beside him.

He looked up, expressionless. "I'm not hungry."

"Well, you have to eat sometime." I put my arm around him, and we both sat there without saying anything for a minute. Then Danny took a deep breath before he began to speak.

"I just don't understand why John had to go back with his wife. He can't even remember her. He was happy here with us."

I nodded. "He was, and he cares about both of us very much. But he still has to try to give his old life a chance. We're both going to miss him, and it's going to be hard for a while, but at least we have each other." I pulled him close and hugged him, and he hugged me back. We stayed that way for a while; then Danny sat up and looked down at his plate.

"I guess it would be a shame to let these tacos go to waste. Let's eat."

I smiled, and we both grabbed our plates and started eating. An overwhelming sense of peace came over me. Men would come and go, but Danny would always be my son. He was home with me now, and that was something positive I could focus on. It had been just the two of us before I met John, and we'd been just fine. We would be okay again; it would just take a little time. Sure, we would miss John; my heart felt smashed in a million pieces, but I still wouldn't change a thing. John had shown me something I never knew existed: true, unconditional love. No matter what happened between us, nobody could take that away.

CHAPTER 40

Over the next week Danny and I settled into a steady routine. He was happy to be back at school, although he wasn't looking forward to doing the work he had missed while he was in the hospital. I was glad to be back at work; it gave me a sense of normalcy that I needed to move on with my life. On Thursday morning, I was sipping my coffee in the staff room, trying to sneak a few minutes to myself before my shift started. There was a small TV in the corner with the news station on, but I wasn't really paying attention until I noticed a picture of John flash onto the screen. I turned the volume up and heard the voice of a female reporter.

"The 'mystery man' is no longer a mystery. John Doe was found in a ditch with a head injury after his car crashed almost a month ago. He was admitted to Sacramento Grace Hospital and had no memory of who he was before the accident. Although his story was all over the headlines, no one came forward claiming to know him—until now. His wife, Julie Moore, recently returned from a trip to Italy, having no idea her husband had been in an accident. The couple has been reunited and are expecting their first child next month. They are currently trying to put together the missing pieces of their life and get to know each other again. John Doe turns out to be Derek Moore, an insurance salesman from New Jersey. He'd recently moved to Sacramento in an attempt to start his business right here. His parents were Doug and Dianna Moore, winners of the big one-hundred-million-dollar jackpot in the California State Lottery. They died a little over two years ago when their house caught fire. The cause of that fire is still unknown. After their untimely demise, Derek inherited the money, most of which he has donated to several charities, including Shriners Hospitals for Children. He has no siblings, and none of his other relatives live in the United States, so that would explain why it took so long for anyone to come forward." Then a woman anchor came on the screen, sitting at a news desk next to a man anchor. She smiled into the camera with one of those phony white smiles. "Well, this was a very happy ending for our mystery man. We will keep you informed on any new developments."

It went on to another story, but I turned the TV off after that. It was just another reminder that John—I mean Derek—was with her now. He and his wife would be welcoming a child into the world soon. People called it a happy ending, but I had to wonder—where the hell was *my* happy ending?

I walked out to the nurses' station, where Lisa stood, looking at me with a sympathetic smile across her face. I could tell that she had heard the news about John and his newly found wife.

"Hi, Jen, how are you doing?"

"I'm doing just fine," I lied.

She took a deep breath. "I'm really sorry about John. I know you really liked him."

"Thanks," I said. "I mean, I guess I should have known someone would come forward sometime."

She nodded. "Well, if it helps at all, Brian just told me he wants to see other people. Men are just big jerks." She sighed. "You can't live with them and you can't live without them."

I nodded in agreement. "Isn't that the truth."

The rest of the day was pretty uneventful. I was happy to find out that Melissa had been discharged. Both she and her unborn baby were doing well. Most of my other patients were pretty simple cases. There was a man recovering from a hernia surgery, a woman who had broken her arm in a waterskiing accident, and a man who had been in a car accident. He had a bump on his head, and in some ways, he reminded me of John. But he didn't have amnesia, and his whole family was there to see him. I wondered how long it would take until I could get through a day without something reminding me of John.

* * * *

Later that night, after Danny was asleep and the house was quiet, I lay there for the longest time, tossing and turning. No matter how hard I tried, I just couldn't fall asleep. I kept thinking about John. I wondered what he was doing at that very moment and whether he might be thinking about me, too. I wondered if he was starting to remember anything about his life before, and if he was happy with her.

I thought about the news segment I had watched earlier that day, and I realized there were still so many unanswered questions. If John was married, then why wasn't he wearing a ring? And why had it taken Julie so long to come forward? You would think that after she couldn't contact him for a couple of days or a week, she would have jumped on the first plane back to Sacramento. I remembered the look on her face when she'd asked me if he remembered anything. She didn't *want* him to remember. There was something about that woman that made my red flags go up, but I couldn't put my finger on it. Then I remembered the newspaper article I had read, and how she had lost her husband in a fire five years ago. That was the same way John's parents had died a couple of years ago. Maybe that was just a coincidence, but it seemed a little strange to me. I wandered out to my computer, clicked on the Internet, and quickly googled Doug and Dianna Moore. Almost immediately an article came up, titled "Fire Takes the Lives of New Jersey Couple." I read on.

Doug and Dianna Moore were a well-liked couple, who spent most of their time giving to others. When they won the lottery last fall, and became instant millionaires, they didn't spend the money selfishly. They put most of it into a fund for their son, Derek, who attends the college of New Jersey, working toward a degree in criminal justice. They also made donations to several schools, which used the money to provide programs to their students who wouldn't have been able to afford them otherwise. "It has helped us to give some of these kids a better education, and we are so grateful," says Mary Connely, teacher at Sunrise Elementary School.

The community was in a state of shock at the news of their untimely deaths. Dianna was just sixty-two and Doug just sixty-three. Investigators have yet to determine the cause of the fire, but they suspect arson. If anyone has information that would help lead authorities to the person responsible, you can make an anonymous tip by calling the number below.

I took a deep breath, taking this all in. What did it mean? There were so many possibilities. I wanted to do something, but I didn't know what. When I looked at the clock, I realized it was after midnight and I had to work the next day. So I tried to put all of those thoughts to the back of my mind, climbed into bed, and went to sleep.

CHAPTER

41

I had promised Danny I would take him to San Francisco that weekend. He'd been through a lot lately, and I knew it would cheer him up. We were both quiet most of the way there, deep in thought. It was no secret that we were both thinking about John, but neither one of us wanted to say it. Then, as we crossed the Golden Gate Bridge, Danny looked up from the book he was reading.

"I saw John on the news."

"Me too," I answered.

Then his expression turned more serious. "Do you think he'll ever come back?"

"I don't know, son."

"His wife is having a baby."

"I know."

"But he loves you. I can tell. He always smiles when he sees you."

I sighed. "Well, some things are just complicated. Even if he does love me, he had a commitment to his wife, first."

Danny nodded, and we didn't say anything more after that.

We had a great day in San Francisco, taking in all the sights and sounds of the bay. But everywhere I looked, I saw John. I could still remember our trip to the city so vividly, as if it had just been yesterday.

That was the day things had changed between us. We had gone from being just friends to something more. It had been one of the best days of my life. And now, as I walked around Pier 39 with my son, I couldn't stop thinking about it. I missed him so much, it hurt sometimes. But then I told myself it was dumb to feel that way, since he had never really been mine to take.

Danny and I had lunch at a nice little cafe with a view of the bay. We went through the aquarium and the wax museum. We topped it all off with dinner at Bubba Gumps'. I made sure to take plenty of breaks in between, so he could rest. I didn't want him overdoing it so soon after his surgery, even though I was the one who had trouble keeping up with him. He really was a great kid, and I felt so lucky to have him. I admired his strength, and I hoped a little of that might rub off on me.

When we were about halfway home, Danny fell asleep, leaving me alone with my thoughts again. I tried to distract myself by playing one of the CDs I had made from iTunes. But then the song "Take on Me" by *a-ha* came on, and I lost it all over again.

When I turned onto our street, I noticed the police car right away. It was parked right in front of my house, and I wondered why on earth it was there. Something about police cars always made my heart jump, even if I knew I hadn't done anything wrong. I pulled into the driveway, and the policeman looked up at me and smiled. Danny yawned and stretched as he woke up; then his eyes widened when he saw the police car.

"Mom, why is there a cop at our house?"

I shrugged. "I don't know, son." We both got out of the car, and the policeman got out of his car and walked over to us. I said, "Hi, officer, can I help you?"

He nodded. "I think so. You're Jennifer Morrison, right?" I nodded. "Yes, that's me."

He cleared his throat. "My name is Jackson Brown; I called you a few weeks ago about the patient who was staying with you."

I suddenly remembered that conversation and how he had asked me to have John call him, but I never had.

"Well, he's not living here anymore," I said. "He is with his wife now." He nodded. "I know. We're doing an ongoing investigation about the cause of his crash, and I was hoping I could ask you a few questions." I gestured toward the door. "Sure, come on in."

I sat in the living room, across from Detective Brown, and Danny went to his room to finish the rest of his homework. There was a little awkward silence, before the detective finally spoke.

"Well, we know now that John Doe is really Derek Moore. But we still don't know exactly how his car crashed that day. It has been totaled now, but we finally got the report back on it. The brake lines were extremely worn, even though the car was brand new. It looks like someone may have tried to cut them. How long have you known Derek?"

"About a month." I still thought it was strange to hear someone call him Derek. To me, he was still John.

Detective Brown cleared his throat. "And in the time you knew him, did you ever get the feeling he might have some enemies? Someone who might want to harm him?"

I shook my head. "No. He is really one of the nicest people you could ever meet." Then I thought for a minute about the way Julie's husband had died, the same way John's parents had. "But you know, there is something kind of fishy about his wife, Julie Moore. Did you know her first husband died in a fire?"

He nodded. "I know. She goes around to schools and teaches about fire safety."

"Well, Derek's parents died the same way," I told him. "And that fire looked like someone might have started it on purpose."

He raised an eyebrow. "Really?"

I nodded. "I just think it's kind of a strange coincidence. And you know, when I talked to Julie, she acted like she didn't want John to remember anything."

He nodded and scribbled something down on a notepad. "What did she say, exactly?"

I pursed my lips together, remembering my conversation with Julie. "It wasn't so much what she said, it was the way she said it. She said, 'He doesn't remember anything from before the accident, right?' And she gave me a look like she was really hoping my answer would be no."

"Anything else you can think of that might be important to our investigation?" he asked.

I shook my head. "No, I don't think so."

He pulled a card out of his pocket and handed it to me. "If you think of anything, you can give me a call."

"Okay, I will."

That night I had a dream. I was hanging on the edge of a cliff, about to fall. John and Julie were both standing above me, laughing. They were holding hands, and he reached out to touch her big, pregnant belly. I screamed for them to help me, but they only laughed even louder. Then Julie came over and stomped on my fingers, causing me to fall. I woke up just before I hit the ground, with my stomach in knots and my heart pounding. After that, it took me a long time to fall back asleep. And when I did finally get to sleep, it wasn't a sound sleep. I tossed and turned for the rest of the night.

CHAPTER 42

"Are you okay, Jen?" Lisa greeted me at the nurses' station Monday morning with a concerned look on her face.

I nodded. "I'm just a little tired. I haven't been sleeping well."

"Well, make sure you get some coffee, then," she said. "It's going to be a busy day. A bus crashed when it was on its way back from Reno, and it was a really bad one. We have five new patients on this floor, seven more in ICU—and those are just the ones that made it. The others weren't as lucky."

I rolled my eyes sarcastically. "That's just great."

When I went to check on my first patient, a young woman named Kristen who had been in that accident, the first thing I noticed was her nasty head wound. She was watching a game show on TV, and she looked up briefly when I walked into the room.

"Hello," I said. "I'm Nurse Jennifer. I'll be taking care of you today. Can you tell me what your pain level is?"

"About a three or four," she said with a sigh.

I jotted that down on her chart and looked up at her, forcing myself to smile. "Let's put a new dressing on that wound." I went to the supply cabinet to get some new dressing, and when I returned to her bedside, I noticed she was crying. I really wasn't in the mood to deal with a crying patient today. I had enough of my own problems to deal with. But I knew it was part of my job. I put my hand on her shoulder.

"Is everything all right?"

She shook her head. "My little girl was with a babysitter, and this was the first time I have ever left her. Now I can't get hold of them, and I should have been home by now. I feel like such a bad mom."

I sat in the chair beside her bed. "I'm sure you're a great mom. Everyone needs a break every once in a while. As much as I love my son, there are times I sure could use a break from mom duty. I'm sure everything is just fine. Maybe the babysitter took your daughter to the park or out to breakfast. I can try to call them again, if you want."

She looked relieved. "That would be great."

For the rest of the morning, I was so busy, everything seemed like a blur. I had tried to call Kristen's house three times, with no luck. I had three more patients who had been in the bus crash, and they all seemed very needy. Maybe they just seemed that way because I had a lot on my mind. There are some days when a person just isn't meant to be at work, especially with a job as draining as mine.

Just before my lunch break, I noticed Mrs. Furguson in the waiting room. She looked kind of lost and confused. Out of all days she could have picked to come to the hospital, why today? I sighed as I walked over to her.

"Hi, Mrs. Furguson. Is everything all right?"

She shook her head. "I'm afraid not. I've been having some chest pain." I nodded. "I see. How long has this been going on?"

"Oh, since yesterday," she answered, but she didn't seem so sure. That was always her catch-all phrase when she was asked how long she'd had something. If it were any other patient, I would have told her to go down to the emergency room. But this was Mrs. Furguson, and she had a habit of coming in with problems that weren't really problems at all.

"Well, it's almost time for my lunch break, but I will see if Lisa can take a look at you," I said.

She smiled a big, bright smile. "Thank you."

I stopped by the nurses' station before I left for my lunch break, and I told Lisa to check on Mrs. Furguson when she had a minute. Then I grabbed the sack lunch I had packed for myself that morning and headed out to the picnic area for a bite to eat. It was much too nice a day to eat inside. My heart stopped when I stepped off the elevator on the first floor, and I saw John standing there. We both stared at each other for a minute, not sure what to say.

"Hi. How are you doing?" he asked. "And Danny?"

"Just fine," I said. "And you?"

He took a deep breath. "I'm all right. This has been a lot to absorb all at once."

"I bet." I looked around, trying to spot Julie, but I didn't see her anywhere. "Where's Julie?"

"She's upstairs for her prenatal appointment." His eyes wandered down to the ground when he said this, as if he couldn't look me in the eye.

"Listen, I'm glad we ran in to each other," I said. "Because I've been wanting to talk to you about Julie."

He looked surprised. "What about her?"

"Well, I don't think she's being completely honest with you."

"Honest about what?"

"Well…" I paused, trying to figure out where to begin. "Did you know her first husband died in a fire?"

He nodded. "Yes, she told me. I really admire her for going around to schools to teach kids about fire safety."

Right away I could tell that Julie had been working hard to get him over to her side.

"Well, your own parents died the same way, and it looks like someone might have started that fire."

He sighed. "What are you trying to get at, Jen?"

"Well, I think Julie might have had something to do with both of them. And I just talked to Detective Brown yesterday. They got the report back on the car you were driving, and it looks like someone might have tampered with the brakes."

He shook his head. "Listen, I know you are hurting right now, and I am really sorry for that, but that's no reason to try to blame this all on Julie. None of this is her fault. She's been trying to help me remember our life together before, and I feel like a horrible husband, because I can't."

I took a deep breath. "Maybe you can't remember because a small part of you doesn't want to."

There was a long, awkward pause before he spoke again. "Well, I think it's up to me to figure that out, don't you?"

I felt like a deflated balloon. "I guess so." Then the tears start rolling down my face, and I looked him in the eye, trying to recapture that feeling we'd once had. "I miss you."

"I miss you too," he said quietly. "And I meant what I said before: I will never forget you. But right now, I have to try my best to move on with my life. I am going to be a father in about three weeks. I really wish that things could be different, but they're not."

I didn't know what to say. I felt more tears streaming down my face, and I wiped them with the back of my hand.

Just then, Julie stepped off the elevator, clutching sonogram pictures in her hand and grinning from ear to ear.

"There you are, Derek." She looked at John and then at me. It was obvious she could sense the tension in the air. "Is everything all right?"

John nodded. "Everything is just fine. Are you ready to go?"

"I sure am. And I have lots of good pictures of the baby."

"Well, I can't wait to see them," he said. Then he looked at me one last time. "It was nice seeing you, Jen."

"You, too," was all that I could say. And they walked off together, and again, I was left standing there alone.

CHAPTER

43

When I came back from my lunch break, the first thing I noticed was that Mrs. Furguson was still sitting in the waiting room, clutching her chest. She looked to be in a lot of pain, and Lisa was running around like a chicken with its head cut off. I walked up to her, noticing how stressed out she looked.

"Lisa, what's going on? I thought you were going to help Mrs. Furguson."

"I've been trying to," she snapped. "All of these new patients have a hundred needs all at once. Steven keeps asking me for more pain medication, even though I told him countless times that it's up to his doctor. Victoria thinks I'm a shrink or something, and she wants to tell me her life story. And Kristen keeps asking about her daughter. Do you know anything about that?"

I nodded. "I have been trying to get a hold of the babysitter all morning, but no luck." I looked over at Mrs. Furguson again, who was now doubled over with pain. "Why don't you go page her doctor? And get someone up here ASAP. I think she might be having a heart attack."

Lisa went off to page doctor Reynolds, and I went to comfort Mrs. Furguson.

"It's going to be all right," I told her. And I almost started to cry again when I realized I was really saying that to myself.

Before I knew it, Mrs. Furguson had been rushed up to ICU, and I went back to tending my patients. Lisa was right about one thing: this group of patients seemed to pull you in all directions. It was hard to keep up, and it made me feel as if I had failed them. I had always been proud that I was a good mom, and a great nurse, and now I felt as if I were neither. The golden rule in the medical profession was to never let your personal life get in the way of your job. I was definitely breaking that rule today, and no matter how hard I tried, I just couldn't stop.

When my shift was finally over, I went up to the ICU to see how Mrs. Furguson was doing. I was hoping for some sort of happy ending to a hectic day, but when I got there, I found Doctor Furguson sitting in the waiting room, and he didn't look very happy.

"Hi," I said as I sat down beside him. "How's your mom?"

He looked up at me and took a deep breath. "She had a massive heart attack and stroke. She's on life support right now, but technically, she's already gone. It's up to me to decide when to pull the plug."

I gulped, trying to take this all in. It seemed impossible to me that such a vibrant old lady was dead. My first thought was that it was all my fault. If only I had responded a little faster, maybe she would still be okay. Instead, I had been wrapped up in myself. I had failed Mrs. Furguson, just as I had failed all of my other patients that day.

"I'm so sorry," I said.

He shrugged. "She had a good life. And I want to thank you for coming to find me. If it weren't for you, I wouldn't have had this time with her. These last few weeks have been the best, and I would do it all over again in a heartbeat."

I sat back in my chair. "Do you think I can go see her? To say good-bye?"

He nodded. "I know she would want to see you. She talked about you all the time, you know."

I smiled. "I hope she had good things to say about me."

"Of course. She told me you were her favorite nurse. So go ahead, she's in room 38."

When I entered Mrs. Furguson's room, it was hard to hear anything but the sound of the machines that were keeping her alive. I sat in the chair next to her bed, and I took her hand. It was so warm, and that made it hard to believe that technically she was dead. I tried my best to keep it together. I knew that was what she would have wanted. She'd never believed in whining and complaining.

"Hi, Mrs. Furguson," I said. "I just wanted to come see you. You were always one of my favorite patients, you know." I took a deep breath, trying to fight the tears. "I owe you an apology. I should have taken you more seriously when you said you were having chest pain. I feel like I failed you, and I am so, so sorry. I've been a little distracted lately. Danny had to have open-heart surgery because of a heart defect I never knew about. He's okay, but I don't know if I am. Do you remember that patient I introduced you to a while back? John, the one with no memory? Well, we were seeing each other for a while. But then his wife came back, and she's pregnant, and I have never felt so alone." I watched Mrs. Furguson for a while, almost expecting her to respond. But I knew that wasn't going to happen. I squeezed her hand and smiled. "Thanks for letting me vent, Mrs. Furguson. See you later." I knelt down and kissed her on the forehead.

After I left Mrs. Furguson's room, I went back to the nurses' station to get my things. I had never felt more exhausted in my life, and I couldn't wait to go home and have a nice, long bath. I grabbed my purse, and was just about to leave, when a young woman came walking up with a little girl.

"Excuse me," she said. "I'm looking for a patient here. I think she was in an accident early this morning. Her name is Kristen Michaels. Do you know who she is?"

I beamed. "Yes. Yes, I do."

When I walked into Kristen's room, she was watching a movie on the Lifetime channel. She looked depressed, but I knew that would change in a matter of seconds.

"Hi, Kristen, how are you doing?"

She sighed. "Okay, I guess."

"Well, I bet you are going to be more than okay really soon," I said. I poked my head out of the room and motioned for them to come in. As soon as Kristen saw her daughter, her face lit up. She opened her arms, the little girl ran to her, and they embraced. It was one of the most beautiful reunions I had ever seen, and it was just what I needed on a day like this.

CHAPTER

44

The next day Danny had a follow-up appointment with his cardiologist. It was the last week of school, so he had early dismissal all week. I picked him up from school during my lunch break, and he was going to spend the rest of the day with me at work. He had brought plenty of books, and his handheld video game, to keep him busy. I felt a little bit guilty for doing this, since I knew he would be bored out of his mind, but I really didn't have any other options.

"So, what exactly is Doctor Carson going to do?" he asked as we stepped into the elevator.

"Well, he's going to check your incision, and he'll listen to that ticker of yours, to make sure it's still ticking."

He laughed. "Well, I know it's still ticking, or I wouldn't be standing here talking to you."

"That's true," I said.

Just then the elevator dinged, and the doors opened.

"Here we are," I said.

We checked in at the reception desk and waited in the waiting room until we were called. Then the nurse weighed him on the scale and took his temperature and blood pressure. Everything was normal. Then we waited for the doctor to come in. Every minute always seems like an hour when you are waiting in a room the size of a shoebox. Finally, there was a knock on the door, and Doctor Carson slowly walked in. He was more handsome than I remembered him, with deep-brown eyes and jet-black hair. His smile was contagious, and I found myself smiling too.

"Hi, how are we doing today?"

"Fine," I said. "His incision looks good, and he's doing just about everything he was doing before the surgery."

He nodded and scribbled something down on his chart. "That's what I like to hear. Well, let's take a look at your incision, anyway, just to make sure. Do you mind lifting your shirt for me, pal?"

Danny cooperatively lifted his shirt. He still had a dressing over his incision site, and the doctor carefully peeled it away.

"This looks really good," he said. "I can tell your mom is taking great care of you." He looked at me and winked, before he re-covered Danny's incision. "Now, let's get a listen." He placed his stethoscope in his ears and held it to Danny's chest. "Can I get you to cough for me?" Danny did, and Doctor Carson nodded in approval. He continued to listen for another minute or so, before he put the stethoscope back around his neck. "Everything sounds really good. Are there any other questions?"

Danny nodded. "Is it all right for me to play baseball?"

The doctor laughed. "I don't see why not. Just be sure to protect your incision. Now, I just have one question for you."

Danny looked at him, puzzled. "What's that?"

"Would it offend you if I offered you a lollipop?" He pulled a handful of brightly colored lollipops out of his pocket.

Danny grinned from ear to ear. "You wouldn't offend me one bit." He picked a red one, unwrapped it, and started sucking on it.

"Okay, we're all done here, but do you mind waiting in the waiting room for a minute, Danny? I want to talk to your mom about something."

He shrugged. "Okay." Then he walked out the door to the waiting room.

"Is there a problem, doctor?" I asked.

He shook his head. "No, not at all. And, please, call me Kevin. Actually, it's something of a more personal nature. On Friday night, the hospital is having an appreciation dinner."

I suddenly remembered the memo I had gotten about a week ago. "Is that really this Friday night?"

"Yes, and I was wondering if you might want to go with me. As my date."

My jaw dropped. I wasn't really expecting anyone to ask me out so soon. I still felt some sort of weird commitment to John, that if I said yes, I would be betraying him. But then I remembered that he was married, with a baby on the way. And besides, I didn't have any plans for Friday night.

"Sure," I said. "I would love to."

The rest of the day was pretty low-key. Most of the patients that had been in the bus accident had been discharged, and Mrs. Ferguson wouldn't be coming in with some sort of ailment. It made the hospital seem almost too quiet. Danny spent the rest of the afternoon in the staff room, reading and playing his video game, and I couldn't stop thinking about my date on Friday night. Sure, it was just a boring old appreciation dinner, but maybe it was just what I needed to move on with my life and stop obsessing about John.

* * * *

Later that night, after Danny was in bed, I went out to the guest house. I hadn't been out there since John had left, and I thought it would be a good time to get rid of anything that might remind me of him. I slowly opened the door and poked my head in; the first thing I noticed was the stifling heat. Of course; the air conditioner was turned off. I opened a window to let a little fresh air in. There was a nice delta breeze tonight, and it felt refreshing as it blew past me.

BLANK SLATE

I looked up, and I noticed the picture still hanging on the wall of John and me that day in San Francisco. He looked so handsome, and we both looked so happy. That seemed like so long ago now, but in some ways, it felt as if it were just yesterday. I could still smell his aftershave, and when I looked toward the bathroom sink, I could see why. There was an open bottle sitting there, and I walked over to replace the lid. Then I looked around. Everything was in its place. It seemed almost too neat, as if nobody had lived there. If it weren't for the picture and the aftershave, it would be as if John had never existed at all.

I took one more look around, and that's when I noticed the piece of paper that was sitting next to the kitchen sink. I walked over and picked it up. It was a note in John's handwriting.

> Dear Jen,
>
> There is so much I want to say to you, but it's hard to find the words. I can't begin to thank you enough for everything you have done for me. Most of all, for being there for me when nobody else was. You took me into your home, and you were there to listen to me when I needed someone to talk to. I will never forget those little moments, and I hope you won't either.
>
> I am sorry that things turned out to be more complicated than I anticipated. Most of all, I am sorry if I led you on or hurt you in any way. It wasn't fair of me to do that, since I had no idea what the future might hold. Then again, who does? Life is full of surprises. I want you to feel free to move on with your life, to see other people. I think we both know deep down that you deserve much better than the life I can give you right now. You deserve to be with someone who can give you his whole heart, not just a little piece of it. It hurts me so much to say good-bye to someone I really care about, but I am only doing

it because I care about you so much. I hope someday you will be able to understand. Please take care of yourself and Danny. And most of all, live your life to the fullest. Be happy. Enjoy all of the little moments.

Love,

John

    When I finished reading that letter, the ink was smeared with my tears. It confirmed everything I knew deep down but hadn't wanted to admit to myself. I knew that John would always have a special place in my heart, and I would have a special place in his. But right now, it was time to let go. I had to move on with my life if I wanted to be happy, and that's exactly why John had written that letter. I carefully folded the letter and put it in my pocket. Then I gently took the picture off the wall. These things would go in a special place where I could look at them when I wanted to remember John. Then I closed the window, turned off the light, and looked around one last time.

    "Good-bye, John," I said. I shut the door behind me and walked out without looking back.

CHAPTER 45

Friday night was the appreciation dinner at the hospital, and I had spent the entire day trying to figure out what to wear. Everything I owned seemed to be either too dressy or not dressy enough. I finally decided on my green skirt, with a cream-colored blouse. I tried it on and admired my reflection in the mirror. The skirt was just the right length. It didn't make me look like a slut, but it didn't give the impression I was a prude, either. Then I went to touch up my makeup and flat-iron my hair. It normally had a little wave to it, but I was in the mood to go straight tonight.

Danny was spending the night at Tommy's house. His mom was taking the boys to John's Incredible Pizza to celebrate the end of the school year, and he'd been looking forward to it all week. It was supposed to be his weekend with his dad, but David had agreed to switch weekends so Danny could go to Tommy's. I was impressed that David was really trying to make an effort to be a better father. He would never be one of my favorite people, but now it was a lot easier to maintain a good relationship with him, which was a good thing, for Danny's sake.

When Kevin pulled up in the driveway, my heart started to race. I suddenly felt like a high-school teenager going on my first date. I was nervous, but I knew all I had to do was be myself. Either he would like me or he wouldn't. It was as simple as that. And if he didn't, then there were plenty of other fish in the sea. One of these days, I was bound to find one that did like me. The possibilities were endless.

Kevin's eyes widened when I answered the door, and he gave me a smile of approval. "You look great."

"You don't look so bad yourself," I said.

"Are you ready to go?"

"Ready as I'll ever be."

Kevin and I were quiet most of the way to the hospital, but then, as we pulled up to a stop light, he turned to look at me. "Can I ask you something?" he asked curiously.

"Sure. What?"

"Were you and that mystery man seeing each other? I mean, were you an item? I saw the story on the news, and I was just a little curious."

I thought about this for a moment. I wanted to be careful about how I answered that question, so I didn't set off any alarm bells. I wanted Kevin to get to know the real me, not just the ex-girlfriend of the mystery man.

"Well, we were," I said. "But it's over now."

"Do you still have feelings for him?"

That was a hard question for me to answer. Of course, I would always have feelings for John, but I didn't want Kevin to think I was hung up on him, either.

"I have feelings for him, but not the kind you are thinking of. I care about John, and I always will. Just like I care about all of my friends."

He nodded. "I like that answer."

He drove quietly for a while, and then he looked over at me and smiled. "I'm really glad you came with me tonight."

I nodded. "Me too."

When we arrived at the hospital, the banquet room was decorated beautifully. The tables were set up with flowers and candles, and the smell of good food filled the air. It was a mixture of steak and some kind of dessert. It felt kind of strange somehow to be at work at night, when I wasn't on duty, but it was nice, too. I saw many of my co-workers already seated. Lisa looked up and waved as soon as she saw us, and I waved back. I noticed she was sitting with a man I didn't recognize, and I had to laugh. Lisa seemed to have a different boyfriend every other week.

"There's a table right over there that looks nice." Kevin gestured toward a table in the back.

"It looks perfect," I said.

We walked over to the table together, and Kevin pulled out my chair so I could sit down. Mac walked over to us, with a big smile on his face. He and a few of the other cafeteria workers usually helped serve everyone at the appreciation dinner.

"Hi, Jen," he said. "Hello, Doctor Carson."

"Hello," we said in unison.

"Can I get you started with something to drink?"

Kevin looked over the drink list. "How about a couple of glasses of your best wine?" He looked over at me. "Is that all right, Jen?"

I nodded. "Sounds good to me."

Mac smiled. "I will have that up in just a minute. And you guys are in for a treat tonight. There's going to be good food, live music, and a drawing for some really cool prizes, too. Make sure to get your tickets over there at that table." He pointed toward a table in the back. A woman who I recognized from Accounting sat there, handing out tickets.

"I think this is going to be a really nice evening," Kevin said with a smile.

We had a really great time that night. Kevin told me a little more about himself. I learned that he came from a large family, with eight siblings. I wondered how his mother had managed so many kids all at once. He told me that he had decided he wanted to be a surgeon after he'd done some volunteer work at a hospital when he was in high school. He had never been married, but he had come close a time or two. He was ready so settle down if he met the right woman, and he was trying to overcome his shyness, so he could put himself out there in the dating world. It was refreshing to be with someone who could tell me about his past.

"And how about you, Jen? he asked. "I have been going on and on about myself, and I just realized I haven't given you a chance to tell me about *your*self."

I laughed. "It's okay, really. There's not much to tell. My life isn't exactly exciting; it's just ordinary."

"I like ordinary," he said with a smile.

"Well, I'm an only child, so my house was probably a lot quieter than yours was, growing up. My parents were very devoted, but my mother and I did butt heads, sometimes. I think we were both just too stubborn for our own good. I didn't know I wanted to be a nurse until I was in college. My college roommate had an epileptic seizure, and I had no idea what to do. That's when I realized I wanted a career that I could really make a difference with."

He nodded. "And you do. I have heard you are really great at your job. You really put your heart into it, and that's rare these days."

"I guess so." I took a sip of my wine and looked around the banquet room. It was almost full now, and Doctor Martin walked past us and sat down at the table next to ours.

"So, tell me about Danny's father," Kevin said.

"Do you want the long version or the short version?" I laughed. He shrugged. "Whatever you feel comfortable with."

"Well, we married way too young, and that was my first mistake. Then, when we started having trouble, I thought a baby would fix it all. That was my second mistake. But I learned from all of those mistakes, and I think I'm a stronger person because of it."

"I can tell," he said. "So, do the two of you get along now?"

"Yes, it's actually gotten a lot better since Danny had his episode on the baseball field. I think it really made David have a reality check. Before that, he was threatening to sue me for custody of Danny, and take him to New York."

He raised an eyebrow. "Really?"

I nodded. "But I knew he was never really going to do it. He's kind of like a balloon, all full of hot air."

Just then, the chief of staff stepped up to the podium to speak.

"Ladies and gentlemen, thank you for joining us tonight. We are here to pay tribute to some of the most important people in our community. Our doctors and nurses have put in many long hours to ensure that our patients get the best care possible. They have sacrificed time with their own families so that complete strangers can have more time with theirs. Words can't express how vital these people are to the patients they care for. And this dinner, and a little certificate, probably can't do that, either, but it's a start. So, everyone, enjoy your dinner. This is for all of you."

The rest of the night went better than I could have imagined. The food was fabulous, the music was great, and Kevin and I got along so well it was if we'd known each other for a long time. I received a certificate of appreciation for exceptional patient care and won a gift basket with assorted chocolates and movie passes. But still, I felt as if something were missing.

On the way home that night, Kevin and I were both quiet. We didn't say much until we were right down the street from my house.

"I had a really good time tonight," he said.

"Me too," I answered.

"So, do you think we can go out again? Maybe we could go somewhere that's not work related this time."

I smiled. "That would be nice."

As we drove closer to my house, I noticed there was someone sitting on the front porch. It was a man, sitting with his head down. It wasn't until Kevin pulled up in front of the house that I realized it was John.

Kevin and I both stared in silence for a moment, not knowing what to say.

"Isn't that the mystery man?" he asked, leaning in to get a closer look. I nodded. "Yes, that's him."

He patted me on the shoulder. "Listen, Jen, I had a really good time with you tonight, but I can tell you have some unfinished business with him. So go ahead and talk to him. No hard feelings."

I took a deep breath. "I really don't know what to say."

"You'll figure it out." His words gave me the confidence I needed.

"Thanks." I grabbed my gift basket and started to step out of the car.

"No problem. And Jen?"

"Yes?"

"If things don't work out with you and the mystery man, you have my number." I smiled as I closed the car door behind me, and I watched him drive away.

As I walked toward John, everything seemed to be moving in slow motion. He was just sitting there, staring into space.

"John, what are you doing here?"

He continued to look forward, expressionless. Finally, his gaze met mine. His eyes were sad, and he looked just as lost as the first day I had met him in the hospital.

"Are you okay?" I asked.

He took a deep breath. "I remember everything now."

CHAPTER

46

John and I sat side by side on the front porch for a long time, neither of us saying anything. My heart raced with anticipation as I waited for him to speak. I knew that whatever he'd remembered would probably change everything. When he finally opened his mouth, he didn't say what I expected him to.

"Did you have a good time tonight, with Doctor Carson?"

I nodded. "It was a nice evening. I got a certificate and won this gift basket." I motioned toward the gift basket that was sitting beside me.

He smiled a weak smile. "Good. I'm glad you had fun."

We were both quiet again, and then he cleared his throat. "I don't know where to begin," he said.

I shrugged. "You can start from the beginning, and take as much time as you need. Danny is sleeping over at Tommy's, and I don't have to work tomorrow, so we have all the time in the world."

"First of all, I want you to know how much I have missed you. I know I acted like a jerk the other day at the hospital, and I want to apologize for that. I have been confused ever since Julie came back, but everything is so clear now. And you were right about everything."

"I've missed you, too." I paused for a minute while I thought about what to say next. "I got the letter you left for me."

He shook his head. "I was wrong. I wasn't thinking clearly when I wrote that letter. It was the day Julie came back, and I thought I was doing what was best for both of us. I thought you would be better off without me, but now I know that isn't true. So I want you to tear that letter up and throw it away. Forget everything I wrote in it."

I took a deep breath and felt my heart start to race again. "You've got me really curious now. What exactly do you remember?"

There was a long pause, and then it all came out.

"Julie lived in my neighborhood when I was growing up; I think she moved in when we were both in third grade. She always had a crush on me, but I never felt the same way about her. This went on for years, all the way through high school. She got really jealous when I asked Rachel to the homecoming dance. I tried to tell her that, even though I thought she was a really nice girl, I just wasn't into her that way. Anyway, when it was time for college, she decided to study abroad, and I went to the college of New Jersey. I wanted to stay close to home, and she wanted something different, I guess. So I didn't see her for years." He let out a sigh and buried his face in his hands.

"It's okay," I assured him. "Take all the time you need." I noticed his lips looked a little dry. "Can I get you something to drink?"

"Some water would be great," he said.

I went to the kitchen and returned with two glasses of water. I handed him one, and I took a drink from the other.

"Thanks." He took a long drink, and then he continued with his story.

"So I didn't see Julie for ten years, and then my parents won the lottery. You've probably heard the story on the news about how they were millionaires, right?"

I nodded. "Yes. I also heard they donated a lot of it to charities."

"That's right," he said. "They always wanted to help others. They really were the kindest people you could ever hope to meet. Even after they had all that money, they stayed in their house in New Jersey. They said there were a lot of people who had it a lot worse than they did. I was really lucky to have them as parents. I had thought about going away to college, but I'm glad that I stayed close to home. I wouldn't give up one minute I had with them." He tapped his fingers on the side of his water glass. "So, anyway, soon after they won, Julie came to town to visit her parents. She hadn't changed much, and she made any excuse she could to spend time with me. She was always coming over to borrow milk and eggs, or she'd offer to walk the dog. It seemed, in some ways, like she was even *more* obsessed with me. And she was always asking questions about my parents' money. I thought it was just her way of making conversation, but now I know better. She was on summer break from her teaching job at the time, so she stayed around for a couple of months. I had a part-time job as an insurance salesman. I guess you could say I never quite knew what I wanted to do. I had my degree in criminal justice, but that fizzled out once I did my internship at the police station. So I was at work the night my parents' house caught on fire. I came over to see them after work, just like I always did. There must have been a dozen fire trucks and police cars. There was nothing left, and when they told me my parents were dead, I didn't want to believe them." His eyes started to well up with tears, and I grabbed a tissue out of my pocket and handed it to him. He wiped his eyes and reached over to take my hand. "Thanks."

"You're welcome. I really am sorry about your parents. That must have been tough."

He nodded. "It was probably the darkest time in my life. I still miss them so much it hurts sometimes. I really wanted to believe that the fire was just an accident, even when the police suspected arson. I couldn't fathom someone doing something like that." He shook his head. "But Julie was always there when I needed to talk. I thought she was just being nice, but now I have a feeling she had another motive. I couldn't stay in New Jersey anymore, because everywhere I looked, I saw them. There were just too many memories. So I traveled a lot, looking for a new job and looking for a new place to fit in. I came here to Sacramento for a while, and that's when I met Sarah, the woman we saw at the restaurant that night. I was really in no mental state to be in a relationship, so when I left, I didn't leave a note or say good-bye. It was really a crappy thing to do, and I'm not proud of it. Julie and I kept in touch over the phone, and when I went back to New Jersey, we got together one night. I told her I was probably going to move, that staying there where I had grown up was just too hard. She begged me to stick around—it turns out she had moved back to New Jersey, and she had a new teaching job. I still wasn't sure if I wanted to stay, but we went to a bar that night and both had a little too much to drink. We ended up at a little chapel. The next day when I woke up, I was shocked to find out we were married. I wanted to end it right away, but Julie begged me to give her a chance. I had never been married before, so I figured, what do I have to lose?" He exhaled before he continued.

"Things were all right between us for a while, but I never really felt that spark with her. I probably wasn't the best husband in the world. I traveled a lot and left her alone, but she never complained. It was still hard for me to be in a place where my parents' memories were everywhere, and I really wanted to move. Then she told me she was pregnant."

I took a deep breath. I almost wanted to forget about the little person that wasn't even born yet. I felt mean for thinking that way, since the baby hadn't done anything wrong. "What are you going to do about the baby?" I asked quietly.

"Well, I was just getting to that. Julie and I decided that if we were going to move, we should do it before the baby was born. We decided to move here, and we bought a really great house in Granite Bay. My parents would probably roll over in their graves, because this house was just a little extravagant. It wasn't exactly my taste, but I was trying to impress Julie. I also bought the Mercedes, the car I was driving when I was in the accident. Then I started having some doubts. I'd always thought the timing was a little off, and in the back of my mind I knew that baby wasn't mine. I went with her to the doctor for one of her routine appointments, and that's when I found out her due date was

August fifteenth, not the end of September, like she told me. There's no way that baby is mine. I was out of town at the time, on one of my trips. When I confronted her, she admitted the real father was an old friend of mine back in New Jersey. I was angry and hurt, but also relieved. I knew we weren't right together. Then I started thinking, if she would lie about that, what else was she hiding? I remembered that when the police were investigating the fire, they'd found a barrette. I didn't think anything of it at the time, but I found a matching one in her drawer. I confronted her about that, too, and that's when she blew up. She told me that I didn't know what I was talking about, and there were a million barrettes just like that one. I could tell by the way she was acting that she was guilty. I knew her well enough to know that she had this nervous tick when she was lying about something. Her eyes would blink really fast. So I called her on it. I told her she was lying, and that she would pay for what she had done to my parents. I took off my wedding ring and threw it at her, and then I turned to leave, but that's when everything went black. The next thing I remember, I was in my car on the highway, heading in the wrong direction. I panicked, and I tried to use the brakes to slow down a little, but they weren't working right. I remember being so terrified, like I just knew it was the end. Then a huge semi truck was heading right for me, and that's when I swerved and crashed."

We both sat there in silence again, neither one of us knowing what to say. It was so much for me to take in all at once, and I couldn't begin to imagine how John was feeling.

"When did you remember all of this?" I asked.

"It started coming back in little bits and pieces yesterday," he answered. "Julie doesn't know I remember everything yet. I wanted to keep her in the dark just a little bit longer, while I decide what to do. I really think she had this whole thing planned for a while now. She set my parents' house on fire because she knew I would get the money. She tricked me into marrying her because she knew I was rich. Then she tampered with the brakes and sent me into oncoming traffic, hoping I would die and she would be next in line. Her first husband was also wealthy, and she became an instant millionaire after he died. No matter how much she has, it's just never enough."

"What are we going to do?" I whispered.

"I don't know," he answered. "This would be a lot for anyone to take in, and I don't expect things to be just like they were before. I know a lot of damage has been done, and it's going to take some time. But now that I remember everything, I can honestly say that I love you more than I have ever loved anyone. Maybe I wasn't ready to be in a relationship before, but I'm ready now. I want nothing more than to be with you; I just hope I'm not too late."

I shook my head sadly. "Well, I did have a good time with Doctor Carson tonight, and you do have a lot of baggage. Do you have any idea how heartbroken I was when you left? And Danny was beside himself."

He took a deep breath. "I thought you might feel that way. All I can say is I'm really sorry. I guess I should go; I really shouldn't have put that all on you like that."

He started to stand up, but I reached out and grabbed his arm to stop him. "Wait a minute," I said. "You didn't let me finish."

He sat down, a weak smile across his face. "Okay, finish."

"Well, I don't think it would have hurt as much if I didn't love you back. And maybe I had a nice time with Kevin tonight, but the whole time, I kept thinking about you. Whatever problems we need to deal with, we will deal with them together."

Now he was smiling from ear to ear. "How did I get lucky enough to find you?"

I shrugged. "I don't know, but you better hurry up and kiss me before I change my mind."

With that, he scooped me up in his arms, and we kissed under the moonlight, never wanting to let each other go again.

CHAPTER

47

When I woke up the next morning, I felt surprisingly refreshed, even though I'd only had a couple hours of sleep. John and I had stayed up until the wee morning hours, talking about anything and everything. I learned more about his life when he was growing up in New Jersey. He told me he had never gotten very good grades when he was in school, and that he had loved to sneak out at night and play pranks on some of the neighbors. I felt that I knew him better now, and it made our relationship seem so much more real. I shared more about my younger years, and we discovered that we actually had a lot in common. Then we fell asleep in each other's arms, completely content.

* * * *

John's eyes fluttered open, and he looked over at me. "Good morning, beautiful."

"Good morning," I said back.

He wrapped me in a warm embrace. "You know, I could get used to this." I smiled. "Me too."

Then, I heard the front door open and the sound of footsteps coming from the kitchen. "Mom, where are you?"

I took a deep breath and looked over at the clock. "Danny. He's home early."

"Good," said John. "I can't wait to see him."

I jumped out of bed and threw on my robe; then I knelt down and kissed John. "You wait here until I call you. He's going to be so excited."

He nodded, and I walked out to the kitchen, where Danny was rummaging through the cabinets, looking for something to eat. Open-heart surgery sure hadn't slowed down his appetite.

"Hey, sweetie," I said. "Did you have fun at Tommy's?"

He nodded. "I sure did. I even won this basketball at Incredible John's. Did you know there's a roller coaster and everything?"

"That's what I heard," I answered. "Well, I have a little surprise for you." He looked stunned. "Really? It's not my birthday."

"This isn't that kind of surprise," I said. Then I looked toward the stairway. "You can come in now."

John peeked around the corner and slowly walked into the kitchen.

Danny blinked, and rubbed his eyes.

"John?"

"Yep, It's me buddy."

Danny squealed with delight and ran up to give John a hug. "I've missed you."

"I've missed you too, little man."

Then Danny's expression turned more serious. "Are you here to stay?"

John nodded. "As long as you and your mom want me here."

Danny was silent for a moment. "Can I ask you something?"

John nodded. "Sure, anything."

"Do I call you John or Derek? Because the news people said your real name is Derek."

John grinned, relieved that he'd asked such a simple question. "Call me John. That's who I am now. As a matter of fact, I'm thinking about getting it legally changed."

The three of us had breakfast together, laughing and talking just as we used to, without a care in the world. It was easy to forget we still had a lot to do before we could truly be a family. By now, Julie was probably looking for John. I almost had to laugh when I imagined her frantically searching for him. But the reality was, we had to do something fast, before she did. If she was really responsible for murdering her first husband and then John's parents, as well as trying to kill John, then who knew what else she might do? One thing was for sure—we had to be very careful about how we planned our next move.

After breakfast we all cleaned up the mess together and then we went out to the backyard, where John and Danny drew out blueprints for the shelves they planned to add to the tree house.

"These are going to look great," said Danny. "I can't wait to put them up."

John laughed and tousled Danny's hair. "You're a lot like your mom, you know that? Everything has to have its place."

Danny shrugged. "I guess so."

John paused for a minute, looking back down at the paper. "I have a few things to take care of this morning, but I will come back later today, so we can get started on this, okay?"

Danny wrinkled up his eyebrow, something he only did when he was worried. "Promise?"

"I promise." John looked him in the eye to let him know he was sincere, and Danny relaxed a little. He ran off to play in his tree house, leaving John and me alone. He sighed and wrapped his arms around me, nuzzling me gently. "I never want to leave you again, but I think we both know I have to face the music sometime."

I nodded. "Have you figured out what you're going to do?"

"Not exactly. I think I will go to the police first and tell them what I know. Then I will go to Julie and tell her it just isn't working out between us, and I want a divorce. I don't think I will tell her I remember anything quite yet; that should buy us some time. She's probably going to freak out, but at least she won't think of me as a threat."

"Do you need me to go with you to the police station, for moral support?" I asked.

He shook his head. "No, I really think this is something I have to do by myself. I promise I will call you when I'm finished. I have my cell phone back, so you can call me, too. I left the number on the little notepad by your bed."

"Okay," I said. "Good luck."

"Thanks, I'm going to need it."

John said good-bye to the pair of us, promising he'd be back later that afternoon. I had knots in my stomach when I thought about what he was about to do. I felt helpless just sitting around while he put himself in danger like that. But I told myself that everything would be all right, and John would return, just as he'd said he would. And when he did, it would be the beginning of something amazing.

CHAPTER 48

When five-o-clock came around and there was still no sign of John, I was beginning to get a little bit worried. I tried to call the number he had left for me, but it went straight over to voice mail. I paced around the house nervously, trying to tell myself that everything was all right, but I somehow knew that it wasn't.

Danny had spent most of the day playing in his tree house, only coming in to grab a sandwich for lunch. He was happier than I had seen him for a while, clearly thrilled to have John back. He had no idea what John was really doing, or that he might be in danger. I wished I didn't know, either, because then I might be able to relax. Instead, I kept thinking about all of the possibilities. What if Julie had gone crazy after he'd told her it was over? She might have hurt him, or worse. I tried to call his cell phone one last time and when it went to voice mail again, I got a strange feeling in the pit of my stomach. I knew something was wrong, and I couldn't just sit around anymore. I had to do something.

Along with the phone number, John had left an address. I picked up that little piece of paper and walked over to my computer. I quickly typed in Google maps and printed out a map from our address to the one that John had left. Then I stuffed it into my purse and ran out back to get Danny.

"Danny, I need you to come with me for a minute," I called. "I have a few errands we need to do." When he didn't answer, I assumed he was either ignoring me, or he had his iPod stuffed in his ear. I was always nagging him not to play his music so loud; sure it would make him deaf. But like most kids, he never listened to me. I started to climb up the stairs to the tree house. "Danny, we really need to go."

When I poked my head through the door, the tree house was empty. "Danny! This isn't funny!" I backed down the steps slowly, careful not to lose my balance. Then I turned around and saw her standing there. It was Julie Moore, with a smirk on her face. I was shocked to see her, and my heart started racing.

"Danny's not here right now," she said.

Right about then, panic and fear took over my whole body. I could feel my heart beating out of my chest.

"Where is he?" I demanded. "Where's Danny?"

She sighed. "I think that's the least of your worries right now, Jen."

"You better tell me where he is, or—"

"Or what?" she asked. "You wouldn't hurt a pregnant woman, would you?" She caressed her humongous stomach.

I crossed my arms over my chest. "I just might."

That's when I lunged after her. I pinned her against the tree, surprised by my own strength. "Where is my son?" I screamed into her face.

I expected her to be afraid, or at least a little bit intimidated. After all, that's what a normal person would do. But she just looked at me with a calm smile. Then she reached into the pocket of her maternity dress and quickly pulled something out. I felt a sharp pain in my arm, and that's when everything went black.

CHAPTER

49

When I woke up, I felt strange. I tried to move, but I couldn't. There were trees all around me, and a gentle breeze tickled my nose. It took me a while to remember what had happened, and when I did, I tried to scream, but no sound came out. That's when I realized there was tape over my mouth. When I tried to move my arms, they wouldn't budge; they were tied behind my back. Then I heard the sound of someone else struggling, and I was able to turn my head just enough to see Danny lying there. He was tied up, and there was duct tape over his mouth. He was struggling to free himself, the tears streaming down his face. Next to him was John. He wasn't tied up, but he was unconscious. I struggled more, trying to loosen the rope that was tied around my arms. I wanted to comfort Danny as I had when he was younger and had had a bad dream. But I knew this wasn't a dream, and it would take a lot more than some monster spray and a nightlight to make everything okay again.

All of the sudden, Julie appeared over me. She was holding a shovel, and she had the same creepy smirk on her face. "It's probably not a good idea to struggle, Jen," she said. "I gave you a very strong sedative, and it's going to take a little while to wear off."

I tried to scream again. I wanted to tell her to let us go, right now. I had a very strong urge to beat her into a bloody pulp. But when I opened my mouth, no sound came out. I saw Danny out of the corner of my eye, and he was crying harder now. His eyes were bloodshot, and tears streamed down his face like a raging river. He looked so small and helpless, more afraid than I had ever seen him. I wanted so badly to go to him and tell him everything was going to be all right, but I couldn't. Tears started to well up in my eyes, too. I had never felt so helpless in my life.

Julie rolled her eyes. "Stop crying. Don't you know you're only making this harder on yourself? She paused, briefly looking over at Danny and John before she turned her attention back to me. "This really can't be that much of a shock to you. Do you honestly think I would let you just steal my husband away from me, without any consequences? He was mine first, and I'm entitled to what's mine. I do accept my part of the blame, of course. I should have done something that was more of a sure bet. Maybe a fire, or an explosion. A bullet through the head might have done the trick. Oh well, live and learn, right?"

I just glared at her; it was the only defense I had right then. She turned her back on me and walked away, gripping the shovel tightly. Then she started to dig, and I realized there were three huge holes, each one easily big enough for a person to fit into. My heart just about stopped when I realized they were graves and she was going to bury us alive.

Julie was busy digging for a while, but she had to take a break every few minutes. She grabbed her stomach, looking as if she was in a lot of pain. I wondered if she might be having contractions. After all, she was nearing the end of her pregnancy. But she wasn't my main concern at the moment—I was more worried about Danny and John. I looked over at them. They both looked so helpless, and I had no idea what to do. Danny just sobbed quietly, and John hadn't moved at all since I had woken up. I began to wonder if he was still alive, and then I noticed his chest rise. I let out a sigh of relief, but a million thoughts raced through my head. Where was I, anyway? I looked around, trying desperately to spot something that I recognized, but all I could see was a bunch of trees that all looked alike.

Just then, Danny started flopping around like a fish out of water. He was trying to free himself from the rope that was tied around his arms and legs. Julie turned around and walked over to us.

"What do you think you're doing?"

Danny just glared at her and continued to squirm around. Julie was clearly annoyed now, and her expression changed quickly to one of anger.

"Stop that!" she yelled. "Do you really think you're going anywhere? You know, you can blame your mommy for this. She's the one who stole my husband. If she had just walked away in the first place, none of this would have happened."

Danny was quiet now, a look of submission across his face. I felt a horrible guilt that I had put him in danger. It had been selfish of me to put my own needs ahead of everyone else's. Now we were all going to die because of it. I should have listened to that little voice in my head that had told me this was trouble. I should have walked away from John while I had the chance. Then I looked over at him, so pale and lifeless, and I realized he was just a victim, too. He hadn't asked for this any more than I had.

A look of pain came across Julie's face, and she grabbed her stomach. "You're not supposed to come for another three weeks," she hissed. This time, it took her a while before she was able to get back to digging.

I just sat there, trying to come up with a plan that would get us all out of this place alive. I could see that Julie's contractions were getting closer now; that just might distract her long enough for me to free myself. But then, where would I go? I looked around for an escape route and spotted a path. Maybe it led to a main road, where I could get help. Then I realized that help might be closer than I thought. I could feel my cell phone in my pocket, and I worked to stretch my hands out far enough so I could reach it. I breathed a sigh of relief when I held it in my hand, and I felt the numbers, and started to dial. Nine-one-

"What in the hell do you think you're doing?" Julie snapped, and she snatched the phone out of my hand. She ripped out the battery and threw the phone against a tree. It broke into pieces as it fell to the ground. "Nobody is going to help you." She pulled a syringe out of her pocket. "I think it's time to go to sleep now. Only this time, you won't be waking up."

She grabbed my arm, but I lunged around so she couldn't stick me with the needle. Danny was in full panic mode now, his face beet red, and I could hear his muffled screams. Out of the corner of my eye, I noticed John starting to move, and his eyes fluttered open. The needle came closer, almost piercing my skin, and my racing heart banged wildly in my chest. I saw John scramble to his feet. He staggered over to Julie and lunged after her. They fought desperately over the needle, back and forth. John struggled to pry it out of her hand, but she turned it toward him. She was stronger than I'd imagined, and she fought tooth and claw. I heard John scream loudly, and I thought she had stuck him with the needle. But he shoved her down with all his might. She fell backward, a shocked expression on her face. The syringe flew through the air and landed in a nearby bush. Julie was now screaming in pain, unable to get back on her feet.

John knelt down beside me and quickly ripped the tape from my mouth. It stung, but I was relieved to have it off. "Are you okay?" he asked breathlessly.

"I will be," I said, careful to keep my eyes on Julie. John started working on the rope that was around my arms.

"I am so sorry," he said. "I never thought she would do something like this."

Julie was now in full-blown labor, writhing around on the ground and moaning in pain. As soon as I was free, John and I went to Danny and worked together to untie the rope around his arms. It was so tight it had

cut into his skin. As soon as we ripped the tape from his mouth, he looked over at Julie with a horrified expression. "Mom, what's wrong with her?"

When I turned toward Julie, I noticed she was lying in a puddle. Either her water had broken, or there was a leak coming from her dress. She was terrified, and she looked up at me with a pitiful expression.

"Help me. Something's wrong."

"Why should I help you?" I snapped. "After everything you've done, you don't deserve it."

She took a couple of deep breaths, probably something she'd learned from a childbirth class. "Maybe I don't, but this baby does. He didn't do anything wrong, did he?"

I thought about that for a minute. "I guess not."

"And you're a nurse; you must have taken some kind of oath, right?"

I sighed. "All right, let's take a look at you." I took a peek under her dress and made a decision. "It looks like this kid wants to come right now," I said. "John, I want you to call 9-1-1." I turned my attention back to Julie. "Are there any towels nearby?"

She nodded. "In my car, right over there."

"Danny," I said. "I want you to go to the car and bring me some towels. Hurry."

He nodded and ran toward the car.

Julie looked up at me with a grateful expression on her face. "Thank you."

"Well, if you think this is getting you off the hook, you have another think coming," I said. "You do realize that once you have this baby, you're going to be arrested, right?"

"Of course." Another contraction came on, and she doubled over in pain. "Okay, I want you to give a good push."

In all of the years I had been a nurse, I'd never delivered a baby. Sure, I had seen it done, but I'd never had the chance to bring a life into the world on my own. Even under the most horrible circumstances, there's something miraculous about that first little cry. It's the first breath of life—and I'd never heard anything so beautiful. As I held that tiny, squirming baby in my arms, my heart melted. I also felt a little sad, because I didn't know what his fate would be. Who would raise him? Who would be there to share all of his milestones? Every little baby deserved that.

"Is he okay?" Julie asked, a worried tone in her voice.

"He's perfect," I answered. Then I looked over at Danny, who sat with his hands over his eyes. John sat beside him, patting his back for comfort.

"It's all right, Danny," I said. "You can look now."

He removed his hands and slowly walked over to where I sat holding the baby. Then a smile came over his face. "He's kind of cute."

I nodded. "Yes, he is."

John smiled. "You did a great job."

"Thanks." I looked at Julie, who was holding out her arms.

"Can I hold him?"

I placed the baby across her chest. Right after that I heard a siren, and the ambulance pulled up. Two paramedics jumped out and raced over to us.

"Looks like we're a little late," one of the men said.

I laughed. "No, you're just on time."

Then both men looked over at the graves that Julie had been digging. "What happened here?"

I walked over to Danny and John and put my arms around both of them. "It's a long story, but everything's going to be okay now."

CHAPTER 50

I've learned that in life things don't always go as planned. Most of the time you are completely surprised by the way things turn out. There was a time when I'd thought I would be with David forever, but that seemed like a million years ago, now. I never imagined I would meet someone like John. He couldn't even remember who he was when I first met him, but I'd known there was something special about him, and I'd been right. He had had a very complicated past, one that had put all of our lives in danger. Most people would have run the other way without looking back, but I'm glad I didn't. Even after everything we'd gone through, I'd still do it all over again!

The police questioned all of us before they took us to the hospital for evaluation. They were respectful of the fact that we had all been through a great deal that day, so they were as quick as possible, but thorough enough to ask all of the important questions. Julie confessed to everything. I guess she didn't have enough strength to lie anymore. She told them how she'd killed her first husband and then John's parents. She went on about how she'd tampered with Johns brakes, and planned to kill all of us when that had backfired. I had a pretty good feeling she would be behind bars for a very long time.

"You both look great," said Doctor Martin, shaking his head in disbelief.

He was the one giving Danny and me a checkup at the hospital a little later.

"Danny looked at me and smiled. "Were pretty tough, aren't we, Mom?" I nodded. "Yes, we are, and I'm so proud of you. You were really brave back there."

Doctor Martin cleared his throat. "I wasn't finished. You both look terrific for all you've been through, but that was a really strong sedative she gave you. I want you to stick around here for a while, just to be on the safe side, okay?"

I sighed. "All right; I guess we can do that."

A worried expression came over Danny's face. "Mom, I'm hungry."

Doctor Martin smiled. "You can go down to the cafeteria and get something to eat."

Danny and I stood up to leave, and Doctor Martin opened the door for us. "You did a really great job delivering that baby, you know. I'm not sure if I could have done that if I'd been in the same situation."

A feeling of pride washed over me. "Thanks," I told him.

As Danny and I walked down the hall, I noticed doctor Furguson standing there. When he saw us, he looked up and smiled.

"Jen, you're just the person I was looking for! I just saw the story on the news, and I wanted to make sure you guys were okay."

"Were even better than before," I said.

He scratched his head in disbelief. "Why doesn't that surprise me? Listen, while you're here, I wanted to talk to you about something else. I've decided to start a practice here in Sacramento, helping out uninsured people who need medical care. You are one of the best nurses I have ever met, so I would love it if you would come aboard with me. The hours would be long, and the pay would be crappy, but you would get to help out some people who really need it. I'm going to name the medical center after my mom: the Ann Furguson Center."

I paused for a moment. "Well, I don't know."

He raised his hand before I could say any more. "I don't expect you to make a decision right now. Just think about it, all right?"

I smiled. "I'll think about it."

After we had talked to Doctor Furguson, Danny and I continued to walk toward the cafeteria. All of the sudden, Danny turned around, with a look of panic on his face.

"Hey, Mom?"

"What's the matter, Danny?"

"Where's John?"

I shrugged. "I don't know. He went in to get a checkup by the doctor, and I'm not sure where he went after that. But I do have a pretty good idea where he might be. Follow me."

Danny and I took the elevator to the fourth floor, where the nursery was. We both peeked through the window and smiled when we saw the babies all lying in their bassinets. They were so tiny and cute. John was sitting in a rocking chair in the corner, holding a tiny, swaddled baby on his chest. A nurse sat nearby, watching them with a smile. I knew without looking that it was Julie's baby. When he saw us, he smiled and waved for us to come in.

"Well, look at you," I said. "I knew you were great with kids, but I had no idea you were a natural with babies, too."

He sighed. "Well, this little guy had such a rough start, so I figured this is the least I could do. After all, there was a time I thought he was mine. This may seem strange, but I do feel some sort of connection with him, even though he isn't my kid."

"That doesn't sound strange at all," I said.

"I'm glad you've been so understanding, and I'm really sorry for putting the two of you in danger. I should have known Julie was capable of something like that." He paused, and then he looked down at the baby. "You know, I tried to call the baby's father, since I still had his number in my cell phone, but I didn't get an answer. Then I called a mutual friend. It turns out the guy is dead. Some sort of car explosion; it looks really suspicious. I think we can add one more casualty to Julie's list."

"That's too bad," I said. "Every baby deserves a family."

"Yes, and I've been doing a lot of thinking about that." The baby started to cry, and John gently rocked him back and forth. "Maybe we could be his family. I know there is nobody on his father's side or Julie's side that would want to take him."

Danny's eyes lit up. "I could have a little brother?"

A nervous expression came over John's face, and he looked up at me. "Sorry, I shouldn't have said anything in front of Danny."

I smiled, and then I reached over to touch the soft hair on the baby's head. "That's okay. I actually think that's a wonderful idea. I've always wanted another child." Then my thoughts went back to Julie and all of the horrible things she had done, and the hope inside of me turned to fear. "But what if Julie gets out and wants him back? I couldn't take losing him like that."

"I think she's going to be locked up for a very long time," John assured me.

"Do you really think they would give him to us?"

John nodded. "I've already talked to the social worker about it. It's not a sure thing; they do need to rule out any of his biological family that might want him. But it's worth a shot."

Danny and I each had a turn holding the baby, and we debated over names. Maybe we were being a little forward, but I didn't care. I was already in love with this perfect little person. We were having a hard time agreeing on a name, until Danny looked up, with a big grin on his face.

"I think we should call him Derek. That was your name, right, John? But you're not going to use it anymore."

John beamed. "I think that is a great name. What do you think, Jen?"

"I love it," I said.

John stood up, and he gently laid the baby down in his bassinet. Then he turned to Danny and me. "I don't know about you two, but I'm starved."

"We were both thinking the same thing," I said.

John reached out to take my hand, and he put his other arm around Danny. There was no way to tell what the future might hold, but as we walked out together that day, I felt more complete than I ever had. This was my family, and wherever life took us, we would be together.

SIX MONTHS LATER

"We need to leave in about twenty minutes," I called. "This is an important day—we don't want to be late." I heard moans coming from the tree house.

"Aw, Mom, we're having too much fun."

"You two have been in that tree house all day," I said. "What are you up to, anyway?"

"Oh, nothing," John and Danny said in unison, a mischievous tone in their voices.

"Well, whatever it is, wrap it up," I said.

I walked into the house and went to the nursery to check on the baby, who was cooing quietly in his crib.

"Hi, sweetie," I said. "Are you awake?" He looked up at me and smiled, his whole body trembling with delight. I scooped him up in my arms and held him close, breathing in his sweet baby smell. I knew that all too soon that scent would disappear.

"This is a very important day for you," I whispered. "This is the day you become a permanent part of this family. What do you think about that?" He smiled his sweet smile again, and I smiled back. I couldn't have loved him any more if he were my own child, and John felt the same way. Danny also relished being a big brother. He taught little Derek something new almost every day.

I went through all the routines necessary when there is a baby involved. I changed him, fed him, and packed his diaper bag. I'd almost forgotten how much work it was to take care of a baby, but I loved every minute of it.

"We're all ready to go," I heard John say as he walked into the nursery. He looked down at baby Derek and made a silly face, and the baby squealed with joy.

I smiled. "Okay, let's go."

All throughout our house, there were now many memories of us as a family. Pictures of the four of us were everywhere. In every one we had huge smiles on our faces, and I knew that was because we were truly happy.

On the mantel, there was a little-league trophy that Danny had won. It was his proof that he had played baseball, even if it had only been for one season.

David and I had a custody arrangement that seemed to work for everyone. Danny would go to New York for a couple of weeks every summer, and David would try to come a couple of times a year to California to see Danny. I was glad Danny had a better relationship with his father now. I think that, in the end, everything worked out just the way it was supposed to.

Julie Moore would be spending the rest of her life in prison. The police detectives were able to find enough DNA evidence to link her to the murder of her first husband and John's parents. She was also charged with three counts of attempted murder. As for the baby's father, they were still investigating. But we all knew she was responsible for that murder, as well. As far as I know, Julie has only done one good thing in her life. She signed away any parental rights to Derek.

We went to the courthouse that day to sign the final adoption papers. It was an emotional day for me, because I had never thought I would have another child. Now that Derek's adoption was final, a dream had become a reality. My family was complete, and my happy ending had finally come.

That night, there was a dinner in honor of the Ann Furguson Center. We all got dressed up. John and Danny both looked handsome in their suits and ties. I even had a cute little mini-suit with a bow tie for Derek, although he didn't like wearing it very much. I put on my best black dress, along with my favorite diamond earrings and matching necklace; they had been a gift from John for my birthday.

As we entered the banquet room, people were already buzzing around. Lisa and Kevin walked over to us, holding hands. They had been seeing each other for the past couple of months, and it seemed to be getting serious.

"Hi, guys!" she called. "We've got good news!" She held out her hand to reveal a huge diamond ring. "We're engaged!"

"Wow," I said. "That's great news! Congratulations."

"Thanks. Well, it looks like things have worked out for you guys, too." She smiled at Derek and tickled his chubby little belly, but he just sat there with a somber expression on his face. He was probably still mad at me for making him wear the suit. It's funny how, even at that age, they can still hold a grudge.

"So, have you set a date yet?" I asked.

She shook her head. "Not yet. But I really want a big wedding. I'm thinking about the beach."

I nodded and smiled, but a little wave of jealousy came over me. John and I were legally married, but we had never really had a wedding. As soon as his marriage to Julie was legally annulled, we had gone to the courthouse and had a judge perform the ceremony. We'd thought we would have a better chance of adopting Derek if we were married. There had been no reception or celebration. I tried to tell myself that it didn't really matter, but deep down, it seemed it did.

Lisa and Kevin went to find their seats, and then I noticed Melissa and her husband come in. She looked so happy cradling her newborn daughter.

"Hi, Melissa!" I said. "It's so good to see you. I've been wanting to meet this little one."

She held the baby up, so I could get a better look. "This is Hope," she said happily.

"Well, she's beautiful."

"Thanks. You have a little cutie there yourself."

Derek let go of his grudge long enough to give her a little smile.

"Well, I should go find a seat," Melissa said. She kissed the top of Hope's tiny head and walked away, beaming the whole time.

"That's probably a good idea." John said. "It looks like the seats are filling up fast."

I looked over and saw Tommy and his mom walking in. I waved at them, and they waved back. They were one of the many families that had been helped by the Ann Furguson Center. Tommy was now able to get his asthma medication for free, and he was able to do anything any other ten-year-old boy could do. Tommy and Danny were still the best of friends. I was happy that they had each other, and that I had found a friend in Stacy, too.

We got to our seats just as Doctor Furguson stepped up to the podium. He cleared his throat before he spoke. "Thank you all for coming today. The Ann Furguson Center is possible because of all of you."

I heard people start to giggle quietly under their breaths. I thought that was odd, but I continued to listen to Doctor Furguson.

"We have been able to help many people who desperately need medical care, and I know my mom is smiling down on us right now. But that's not why were here tonight, is it, folks?"

The crowd exploded in laughter, and John and Danny had sneaky little smiles on their faces. "What's going on here?" I whispered, but they both ignored me.

"John has really found a place he belongs at the center," Doctor Furguson continued. "Along with his wife, Nurse Jennifer Morrison, he has made the center a little less scary for the patients. Because of his generous donations, the center was able to add on a whole new wing, to serve one hundred more patients. I will let John take over from here. Can you come up here, please, John?"

John slowly walked up to the front and took the microphone. I looked over at Danny, who had a sneaky smile on his face.

"You know what this is about, don't you?"

He nodded. "Yes, but I promised not to tell." I looked up at John, who was smiling at me.

"I just want to thank you all again for coming tonight. But there is one person I really want to thank. When I first met Jen, I was lost. I had no memory of who I was. But she was there for me when nobody else was. She took me in, she became my best friend, and she trusted me enough to allow me to build an awesome relationship with her son. Most of all, she loved me. She didn't have to do any of those things. At any time, she could have turned and walked away, but she didn't. I love her today more than I ever have. She is truly the love of my life, and I can't imagine my life without her, Danny, and Derek." He paused for a moment, before he continued, "Now, as most of you know, we're already married. But we never really had a chance to celebrate it the way it should have been celebrated. Tonight, that's all going to change. Jen, will you come up here for a minute? And bring the boys, too."

My heart was pounding in my chest as we walked up to the front. It seemed as if there were more people now than there had been just a few minutes ago, and when I looked out at the audience, I could see all of our friends and family. My heart melted when I realized they were all there for me. And right in the front row stood my mom and dad, cheering. I wondered how I hadn't noticed them before.

"Well, what do you think?" John whispered. "Too much?"

"No," I said. "Just perfect." John scooped me up in his arms and kissed me, and even though there were over one hundred people cheering in the background, it felt as if we were the only two in the world.

ABOUT THE BOOK

Jen Morrison has always thought of herself as a good person. She is a devoted mom to her son, Danny, and a dedicated nurse. She feels lucky in so many ways, but she's never been lucky in love. Her husband left her and their son years ago. Since then, he has re-married and started a new family. Jen is focused on her son and career and vows not to have her heart broken again. But then a new patient is admitted to Sacramento Grace Hospital, and her life is forever changed. He is brought in after a car accident has left him with a nasty head wound and without a memory. He doesn't have any type of identification with him, and no one seems to know who he is. They call him the "mystery man"; he calls himself John. The two quickly develop feelings for each other, but can their love last when his past comes back for him?

ABOUT THE AUTHOR

I have always loved to write, and publishing my first two novels has been an incredible journey. Since *Blank Slate* takes place in a hospital setting, I did some research on medical procedures. I also talked to some doctors and nurses to get a feel for what a day in the life of a doctor might be like. Even though Sacramento Grace Hospital and all of its characters are fictional, I wanted to make it as realistic as possible.

I have been a day care provider and preschool teacher for over fifteen years, and that has been a great opportunity to observe people with different personalities in a variety of situations. I studied early childhood education at American River College. I took many classes in human development, psychology, and creative writing.

When people find out what I do, they usually ask me how I have time to write, with a young son. I am a mom first, and my family is everything to me. I usually do find some time when my son is napping or after he is in bed at night. Sometimes I can squeeze in a few paragraphs in between episodes of *Dora the Explorer*!

I live in Sacramento, California, with my husband, Jim, my son, Kyle, and my father-in-law. The setting for *Blank Slate* is also Sacramento, although some of the places mentioned in the book are fictional. I have an incredible family, and I love every one of them. As always, my sister Amanda helped, assisting with the editing and development of my book.

www.ingramcontent.com/pod-product-compliance
Lightning Source LLC
LaVergne TN
LVHW041805060526
838201LV00046B/1140